CHRISTMAS MURDER

HILDA MYSTERY SERIES - BOOK 7

MIKE NEVIN

HOWCARING

Copyright © 2024 by Mike Nevin

All rights reserved.

No part of this publication may be reproduced, distributed, or transmitted in any form or by any means, including photocopying, recording, or other electronic or mechanical methods, without the prior written permission of the publisher, except as permitted by U.K. copyright law. For permission requests, contact howcaring.com

The story, all names, characters, and incidents portrayed in this production are fictitious. No identification with actual persons (living or deceased), places, buildings, and products is intended or should be inferred.

First edition 2024

Published by howcaring.com

Contents

Dedication	V
Introduction	1
1. Prologue	2
2. Chapter 2	5
3. Chapter 3	16
4. Chapter 4	28
5. Chapter 5	43
6. Chapter 6	61
7. Chapter 7	74
8. Chapter 8	83
9. Chapter 9	94
10. Chapter 10	105
11. Chapter 11	117
12. Chapter 12	130

Without all my family and friends, I couldn't have finished this book.

Introduction

If you want to see more about the characters, you'll find a character list Chapter 13

Chapter One

Prologue

The Week Before Christmas 1948

Department Store, London, UK

It was hard to see where the blood began, and the red suit ended. One thing is certain; the fur trim on the sleeves should not be red. Father Christmas lay dead in an alley by Carvey Michaels Department Store. Not the actual Father Christmas, of course. I'm sure he was at the North Pole, getting ready for his mammoth Christmas Eve delivery trip. If he'd gone AWOL so near Christmas Eve, his elves would have soon sent out a hue and cry. So this must have been one of his many stand-ins who dress up and entertain children around Christmas time. Being not long after the war, Father Christmasses were in short supply; they could ill afford any losses. But then, who wants Father Christmas dead at all?

...Wait, what? Father Christmas dead? Even if he was just a helper. Surely not in a Christmas book? Christmas is a time of peace on earth and opening presents. Sitting around the wireless and listening to Mrs Dale's Diary on the BBC Light programme. At least that's what they did in the 1940s. Excess eating and drinking would have to wait until rationing ended. While we are discussing Christmas; many people also have this crazy idea that Christmas should be about the birth of Jesus. Something about the origin of the name Christ (Jesus), mass (receiving God's grace), and the reason the Church first hijacked this winter celebration to remember the birth of Jesus. It seemed as good a time as any to remember the birth of the Saviour of the world. Anyway; we don't need to get into a theological debate and we don't want arguments at Christmas. Families have enough of those over the turkey and trimmings. Of course, people didn't have as much food in 1948.

Now, if this is a Christmas murder mystery, cosy or otherwise, we can only kill off a few elves. At the worst, a reindeer can catch a cold. Perhaps a present can go missing? But one thing is certain; no one can die – especially not a cuddly Father Christmas. Let's assume for a moment that the guy was cuddly. Aren't they normally tubby? Or at least they would have a cushion shoved up their tunic to look chubby – even in 1948. So, are we clear? No deaths, especially not that cheery chappy in red – agreed?

***

Now we are all in agreement. Let's get back to the dead Father Christmas.

The jolly chappy, or rather ex-jolly chappy, was lying in a foggy London alley. Did I mention it was foggy? Very foggy. So foggy you could hardly see Father Christmas lying dead in the alley.

Oh dear, there is a death, and it's our favourite man in a red suit. Take a deep breath, have a quick sip of your favourite tipple and let's see if we can at least work out who did it? Then you can sleep easy on the sofa in front of the re-runs of The Great Escape or Mary Poppins. Maybe the real Father Christmas will leave you a little gift. So long as you were good. That'll cheer you up.

Chapter Two

December 1948

Alley by Carvey Michaels, London, UK

There are probably a lot of things you could say about Christmas 1948. But no one could accuse that winter of being a white Christmas; unless you count the dense fog and even that was more of a dark grey. It had been one of the warmest Decembers for many years. One thing is absolutely certain, the Father Christmas lying dead in the alley had not arrived by sledge. Unless it had wheels; anyway, there was no sign of a sledge wheeled or otherwise.

The year before had been one of the coldest on record. Deep snow for months on end; but not 1948. At least the police who would deal with this poor man in red's death would be able to work in comfort — once they finally arrived, that is. Because no one had yet discovered the seasonal body. There was one bit of good news. Father Christmas was not lying on the muddy pavement alone – not that he'd notice, of course. The murderer still stood staring at the body. Maybe that's not great news after all. One wonders why the murderer would still be admiring their handiwork? Perhaps they felt securely hidden by the blanket of fog. Or they wondered if they had overlooked something? This could be their first murder and they were just surprised at what they'd done? Or admiring such a good job. Whatever the reason, they were standing above the body.

A sound caused the murderer to glance up from their wonderful bit of work, then run and hide nearby. Perhaps they planned to watch the unfolding drama as the police arrived. If that was the case; they'd have a long wait yet. The noise had just been a black cat. Aren't they supposed to be lucky? Certainly not for our poor man in red. Now unless Scotland Yard had stooped to employing feline investigators, not much would happen for a while yet. So we'll leave Father Christmas and his murderer in the alley.

A Week Earlier – 1948

Kilburn, London, UK

Sometimes, in order to understand something, you need to go backwards. Not literally, just back in time. So it is with our poor man in red. We must jump back a week and out from the city of London into the district of Kilburn. If you were feeling fit and fancied hopping on a bicycle, then it would take you about half an hour to travel between Kilburn and Carvey Michaels Department Store. No doubt there's also a more direct route;

one that crows take. Given that a murder would happen at that store in a week, asking crows about the distance might be apt. But unfortunately I don't have that information to hand; not having chatted to any crows. But Kilburn is close to the centre of London.

A delightful young couple, Hilda, and Arthur Shilton, live in Kilburn. But they didn't possess a bicycle, nor did they know much about crows. Ornithology not being a passion for either of them. They lived on a fairly ordinary street and had been happily married for two years. Ah, young love. Hilda was a mere twenty-eight years old and Arthur was only a year older. Some of you may well recognise the name Hilda Shilton. In her later life, she travels the globe, solving murders and mysteries. But that future was so far away in 1948, it hardly seems worth mentioning; still the damage is done.

Getting back to the present; or is that the past? Hilda was happily married to Arthur. Perhaps it's as well she didn't know that her dear Arthur would be taken from her in just four years' time. Life can be so cruel. But for now, this wonderful couple enjoyed snuggling up in their two up, two down mid-terraced home, near to Hilda's parents. Pearl, Hilda's best friend, also lived nearby. What a small world. Well, it was in 1948.

Life in the 1940s in Britain was far less mobile than later. Families lived near each other; a mixed blessing. Those wearing rose-tinted spectacles today will tell you how wonderful those times were. Hilda felt rather miffed that her mother and pops. Pops is what she called her father; were always visiting. Hilda had assumed that once married she would have free rein to live as she chose. But her mother would often check that Hilda was 'doing alright.' It never occurred to Hilda that her mother may have a guilty conscience about her own life and her visits were to salve her guilt.

There were some advantages to being in the same area from childhood. Best friends, Hilda, and Pearl, had lived next door to each other since they were eight years old. They went to the same school, started girl guides together, gave up on guides together. Discovered boys were horrible at the same time. Then realised boys weren't all that bad at the same time. Started work together and even did the same wartime job.

Pearl had also been with Hilda on two murders investigations and a mystery Hilda solved. After all, Hilda didn't wait until she was in her seventies to start investigating murders. As far as Pearl was concerned, murders had too much blood, and as for mysteries, they were too mysterious. In 1948, Hilda was married, but Pearl was still single.

***

When people met Hilda and Arthur, they often asked, " How did you two meet?"

This question had an interesting answer that involved the BBC. No, they were not broadcasters, nor entertainers. In fact, Arthur didn't even work there and really Hilda shouldn't have done. But, in 1937 Hilda managed to sweet talk her way into a job as the chief cook at the BBC's Broadcasting House, in Portland Place, London. This job gave Hilda a chance to invite guests as part of the audience to a big band radio concert. The BBC liked to have a live audience to clap and cheer. Hilda invited Pearl and, as fate would have it, the two ladies sat next to Hilda's future husband, Arthur, and great friend, Karl Dansk. Later, they met Lilly, Karl's friend. For Arthur, it was love at first sight. Hilda wasn't convinced about Arthur; until their first dance. After that, it was love at first dance for her. They wanted to marry straight away, but Hilda's parents suggested they wait till after the war. Which they did, getting married in 1946.

***

During the second world war. Arthur worked in the war office, at least that's what he told Hilda. Arthur's actual job was in the secret service, SIS. Hilda's father had recruited Arthur into the intelligence service, soon after Hilda and Arthur met. But during the war, Arthur's work was all desk based. Hilda and Pearl both joined the Women's Auxiliary Air Force (WAAF). There they learnt to drive lorries. It's that experience that gave them the confidence to hire an RV and drive across America in 1997. Mind you, Hilda and driving were never ideally matched. A fact often commented on by her passengers and her son William. During wartime, Karl, and Lilly spent their time entertaining the troops as musicians. Karl became a world famous musician and composer. It wasn't only Arthur and Hilda who married after the war. Their friends, Karl, and Lilly, also got married.

Just after the war, Hilda, and Arthur and moved into their rented house in Kilburn. But Arthur had plans to buy a house in the suburbs. He had his eye on a little village called Stoke Hind; it was rapidly expanding into a commuter zone of London. Little did he know it was a place he would only live in for a short time. But that's another story.

***

Now let's return to Hilda and Arthur in Kilburn. After their marriage, Hilda left her job at the BBC and became a housewife. That was typical of the time and Hilda thought nothing of it. Some at the BBC sighed in relief, because her meals were famous; for all the wrong reasons. One great advantage of being a full-time housewife was it gave Hilda time to pursue her real passion; amateur detective work. She really wanted to solve murders. One should never wish for certain things; they have a tendency to happen. Hilda was about to have her wish come true.

The Week Before Christmas 1948

Alley by Carvey Michaels, London, UK

Poor Father Christmas has waited long enough lying in that muddy and cold alley. Let's get back to him. Just as well he's dead, or he'd get chilly in that drafty place being left all this time. One good thing is that the murderer was no longer standing and staring at the body. Presumably, they had grown bored waiting. Or maybe found a more comfortable place to wait?

Pearl had a day off. Yes, the same day that the man in red had been murdered. She popped round to see Hilda and suggested a shopping trip to central London.

Pearl worked as a secretary in the city. She was clever enough to have gone on to higher levels of training. In fact, she could have easily run the company she sat typing in every day at work. The managing director of the company was more suited to being the cleaner. If he could type, he should have been the secretary. However, his father had owned the company and passed it to his son. So it wasn't about ability for him. Whereas Pearl had skills and natural intelligence, but came from a poor background, life is so unfair. Years earlier, while Pearl was still at school, her dad became ill, and she needed to help look after him. It was too much for her mum on her own. There was little help available, and both Pearl and her mother needed to work in order to pay the bills. So Pearl left school early and had to settle for a basic and frustrating job. Her days off with Hilda became the highlights of her dull existence. In 1948, Pearl was unaware that she would find greater fulfilment in the future.

After meeting up, the two young ladies planned a trip into the centre of London, shopping. Maybe Oxford Street. They had both been saving up for their Christmas shopping. Pearl would be mainly window shopping. For her, the treat was being with Hilda. Pearl wasn't as easily embarrassed as some people. Maybe that's why she was Hilda's best friend. Not everyone could cope with Hilda's dancing and singing in public places.

Kilburn isn't far from the centre of London for two fit young girls and they wanted to save their money for shopping; especially Pearl. So they walked, rather than taking a train or bus. It took them just over an hour to walk; along with a bit of dancing from Hilda. Hardly anyone stared at Hilda as she danced along the pavements. Maybe the people were too embarrassed by the young girl twirling and singing. People in Britain just didn't do that. Except in a musical on stage or film.

***

After a long and wearying trip around the shops, Hilda, and Pearl looked for a place to sit and rest. 'Here's a box to sit on,' said Hilda.

'It's only big enough for one,' said Pearl.

She looked around for another, but there were none in sight. Hilda said, 'That's fine, you take it, I'm going to dance around anyway.'

The box was at the end of an alleyway next to Carvey Michaels Department Store. Pearl sat on the old packing case. Someone had placed it next to the line of waste bins. But the fog hid those from sight. Hilda did a few spins at the end of the alley. These were tricky, with her arms full of bags, and she hit some passing pedestrians; they were not pleased. Hilda stopped, facing the alleyway and said, 'I wonder what's down there?'

Pearl glanced down the foggy alley and said, 'It looks spooky.'

'Nonsense,' said Hilda. 'It looks fun.'

She danced off down the alley. 'Hilda!' shouted Pearl.

No doubt she was remembering all the thriller movies they watched where the heroine headed off into the fog and came to no good. The fog had been increasing in density all day and was now making it hard to see more than a few feet. Passing people appeared without much warning and then disappeared as quickly. The scene certainly looked like a scary movie. From

Pearl's perspective, Hilda was now invisible in the white blanket of fog. Pearl shouted, 'Hilda, are you alright?'

'Don't worry, I'm... oof,' shouted Hilda.

She had tripped over the body of Father Christmas. At least he wouldn't feel it; which is a blessing. Hilda had a good sense of balance and flew over the dead man in red, landing on her feet on the opposite side of him.

'Hilda, what's happened?' shouted Pearl.

Hilda ignored Pearl for a moment and studied the shadowy lump on the ground. 'Whatever is that?' she said.

Pearl stood up, and shouted, 'Hilda!'

But she stayed at the end of the alley, staring at the wall of fog. Then Hilda shouted, 'I'm fine, I think there's a body here.' Hilda bent down for a closer look. 'Yes, definitely a body.'

'A body? Did you say body?' shouted Pearl.

'Gee whiz this is exciting,' said Hilda. 'Yes it's absolutely; a dead body. What a spiffing thing to find.'

Her reaction to dead bodies was not normal, even in her twenties. She loved solving murders. Unlike Pearl, who would rather avoid them, like the rest of us. Pearl took a step further back from the alley, bumped into a passing pedestrian, apologised and shouted down the alley to Hilda, 'I'd better call the police.'

Hilda stared at the body and shouted to Pearl, 'I think it's Father Christmas.'

Pearl shouted back, 'Did you say Father Christmas?'

Pearl moved closer to the alley to hear more clearly. Hilda shouted louder, 'Not the real one of course. He'll be busy getting ready.'

'What do you mean real one?' shouted Pearl.

A passing lady with a dog stopped and stared at Pearl. The lady asked Pearl, 'Are you feeling alright?'

'I'm fine,' said Pearl. 'My friend has found the body of Father Christmas in that alley.'

The lady looked horrified and pulled her dog's lead, saying, 'Come on Alfie, we need to get home quickly.'

Hilda's voice came from the alley. 'Are you still there?'

'Yes,' said Pearl. 'Just getting some odd looks from passers-by.'

'Have you called the bobbies yet?' asked Hilda. 'I'll get the low down on the situation before they arrive.'

Hilda loved the movies and was always trying to copy her favourite movie stars in the things they said. Sometimes she said the oddest things. Pearl shouted, 'I'll do that now. Be careful. I'll be back soon.'

Pearl headed off in search of a policeman on the beat. At that time, officers patrolled the streets regularly, so Pearl was sure she would find one easily. It didn't take her long. A policeman was just walking up Oxford Street towards the Carvey Michaels Department Store as Pearl set off. She bumped into him. 'Watch where you're going young lady,' said the officer.

'A body, Father Christmas, Hilda,' said Pearl, confusingly.

After untangling the confusion and hearing a clearer explanation, the policeman blew his whistle. This summoned nearby officers to join him. Once they had gathered at the scene and discovered it was a murder, they sent an officer back to the police station for further help. A phone call would need to be made to Scotland Yard. The local beat coppers were not suitably qualified to investigate a murder; and this was obviously a murder. At least, it looked like murder. There was blood everywhere. Scotland Yard had the detectives to investigate a murder.

When the policemen had arrived at the murder scene and spotted Hilda near the body, they were so dismissive of female abilities that it never occurred to them she may be gathering evidence. A few policewomen had joined the force. However, other officers did not treat them well. The men attending this murder had no time for the abilities of women. Seeing Hilda; or rather, not seeing her, they totally ignored her, assuming she was a woman of nefarious character. But they were too busy to bother with moving her along. Hilda quietly carried on right under their noses until the officers from Scotland Yard arrived.

Chapter Three

Later The Same Day

Scotland Yard, London, UK

The desk sergeant at Scotland Yard was having a bad day. The week before Christmas was always busy. Too many people out and about celebrating causing public order offences. Thieves running amok making his life a misery. If anything bad was going to happen, this was the time. As far as the sergeant was concerned, goodwill and peace on earth were in short supply at Christmas. He had a queue at his desk that stretched out of sight. When his phone rang, he felt tempted to ignore it. But knew it would just ring again. The blasted thing had been ringing all morning. What fool had placed a telephone on the front desk? It was bad enough dealing with the public face to face.

The sergeant snatched up the phone and said, 'Yes.' Not in a friendly way.

'We need a detective at Carvey Michaels Department Store,' said a voice.

'Who's we?' asked the impatient sergeant.

'Ah, sorry, I'm new at this.' Which, considering the age of the policeman speaking, was true in terms of contacting Scotland Yard. But inaccurate in any other way. The voice on the phone continued. 'Constable Wallis, there's body. Umm, the body of a Father Christmas.' The desk sergeant stared at his phone for a minute. Causing the officer on the line to ask, 'Are you still there?'

'Is this a joke?' asked the desk sergeant.

'No, it's the honest truth, so help me.' The constable crossed himself.

'I'm assuming you mean someone dressed as Father Christmas?'

'Yes, yes, of course, the real one will...' the officer stopped abruptly.

'You were saying?' asked the sergeant, smirking.

'Nothing, said Constable Wallis'

'Right, I suppose you'd better give me the details of this Christmas murder then.'

After hearing the report, the desk sergeant knew exactly who to pass *this* case on to. The man he had in mind was not popular at the Yard and this was a job that would suit him. The sergeant's smile grew. If he had to suffer at Christmastime, so would others. His day had just improved – a lot.

***

People officially called him Chief Inspector Loughty of the Yard. Behind his back, they called him Lanky. The chief inspector did not tolerate fools. Just as well, he didn't have to deal with himself. At the public school his parents sent him to board from age six, Lawrence Loughty became head boy, aged twelve. Not an honour in his view; an obvious choice. Who else would be suitable? He was unaware that his rich parents had bought the honour for him. There would have been little question of him gaining the honour by his own merit. He lacked academic skills and popularity. But his classmates feared him. In the 1940s, people did not frown upon bullying in quite the same way as today. This was a time when corporal punishment was the norm. In public schools, the prefects had the authority to hand out physical punishments. It's no surprise that Loughty intimidated those smaller and weaker than him; which was almost everyone.

As Loughty grew, he became the type of man that no one dared to question. He was tall and muscular, built for fighting rather than thinking. A giant of a man. Goliath comes to mind when describing him. People had to dislike him behind his back. There appeared to be no David to bring him down with a sling. Any challenge to his power was only out of his earshot. Others may have faced mockery or teasing to their face; not Loughty. He developed into his full stature by mid teens. Tall and strong, an obvious, if unmentioned, link to his name. Loughty became a natural leader, strong and certain of himself. People followed him and obeyed. Who would question such a man? Those who did; lived to regret it.

Lawrence Loughty knew his career path from the age of ten. Become the commissioner of Scotland Yard by the time he was forty – at the latest; ideally by thirty-five. Some people are very self-aware, perhaps too uncertain of their abilities. No one could accuse Loughty of that. He was totally unaware of his own limitations. He equated size and power with skill and intelligence. Currently, aged thirty, Loughty felt he was a little behind in his plans. He should be an assistant commissioner by now.

Loughty had joined the police as a constable in 1937. As a constable, he excelled. Criminals took one look at him and crumpled. They didn't want to challenge such a man. He was soon promoted to sergeant. To Loughty's eyes, his abilities had been recognised, and he was on his way to becoming the commissioner. Then came WWII. It had messed up his plans. As it had the plans of many. But at least it gave him a chance to gain some medals. Loughty was in the right place at the right time. While in the army, the enemy wiped out his entire company. They were on a vital mission to hold a key bridge before reinforcements arrived. His was the only George Cross not awarded posthumously. After that, the army promoted him to the now vacant position of captain. They felt he had earned that field commission from his previous post as a lieutenant.

***

After the war, Lawrence Loughty re-entered Scotland Yard and found himself catapulted into a more senior position. The Commissioner of Scotland Yard wanted decorated heroes, especially ex commissioned officers from the services in his senior positions. Thus, Chief Inspector Loughty found himself promoted faster than expected. That is faster than anyone other than he expected. Other officers at The Yard were less impressed with such choices by the hierarchy and saw themselves as overlooked.

Why promote Loughty to Chief Inspector when he had shown no aptitude to the task? But his colleagues kept quiet and bided their time. Perhaps feeling that the lack of detecting experience of men like Loughty would be their downfall. Surely the commissioner would soon see that Loughty lacked such ability. But he was a lucky man and found himself alongside a sergeant with great detective skills. A sergeant who was happy to take a back seat and allow his chief to take the glory. Thus Loughty shone.

***

Chief Inspector Loughty of the Yard sat in his office at the Yard, trying to solve a fresh case. Technically, it was already called New Scotland Yard. Had been since its move to the Embankment in 1890. But moving buildings doesn't change what people call something. It would take a lot longer before the name 'New Scotland Yard' entered the public psyche. Loughty had swivelled his wood and leather captain's chair to face the window. He was on the second floor with a view across the Thames. At least he would have a view if it weren't for the fog. He had been using the misty view to blank his mind and think. Blanking his mind was never hard. Filling it with intelligent thought was the hard part. Loughty had a tricky case to solve. Three bodies, all male, all unrelated and all, stabbed through the heart with a long thin object. He had not been able to pin the murders on any relatives or friends; that's what he liked to do. Look for simple answers; find the obvious culprit and bang them up in prison. Let the lawyers sort out the rest. None of the obvious culprits in this case had a motive or the opportunity. Who else could he look at? His blank mind was still blank.

There was a knock at his door and after being granted entrance, Chief Inspector Loughty's bagman, Sergeant Humblecut, entered. He was an altogether different man to the chief. He was the skilled one in their duo. Humble, as the chief liked to call him in jest, was a thin, nervy man. His school days were ones he had gladly left behind. Bullies similar to Loughty had made his schooldays a misery. Humblecuts army days had also been far less lucky. He had left the army with an injury that still caused him recurring pain; mental and physical. He found life more stressful after the things he had experienced.

As was Humble's way, he entered cautiously. He was a humble man in nature and name; but with a sharp brain. He had gained his position after years of experience and success. If life were fair, he would be the chief inspector or even the commissioner. Humblecut knew how to catch criminals. His methods were slow and methodical. What he lacked was the confidence to put himself forward. As he entered, Humblecut glanced at his boss and said, 'Sir, we've been asked to attend a possible murder on Oxford Street.'

Loughty sprang to his feet and said, 'Right Humble, let's get going. See if we can get this sorted before teatime. Then get back on the other case.'

'Before teatime?' said Humblecut. 'Right.'

Loughty was already out of the door. His sergeant stared at his departing back. 'Don't dawdle,' shouted Loughty from the hallway.

The oddly pared duo headed out of the station. Loughty, a good few feet in height above Humble. They had stopped at the front desk to ask for any further details. But the phoned in report had given the desk sergeant scant information.

Alley by Carvey Michaels, London, UK

It took longer than expected for Chief Inspector Loughty and Sergeant Humblecut to arrive at the scene of the crime. The fog had continued to thicken and was becoming a 'pea souper.' Travelling by any vehicle in such heavy fog was very slow going and potentially dangerous. London at the time suffered repeated bouts of these fogs. Some became dangerously suffocating and caused the deaths of vulnerable people. The damp air and coal fires exacerbated them. Not until the clean air act in 1956 did they begin to reduce.

Loughty and Humblecut walked the last hundred yards after giving up on the slow-moving taxi. Loughty led the way with his longer strides. The fog in the alley had lifted slightly, following an increase in the wind. It was now possible to see five feet into the alley. Loughty arrived at the alley first and entered like a king into his castle. Humblecut followed a few steps behind. Hilda was still checking the alley for clues; out of sight of the two officers. Pearl was back sitting on the box at the end of the alleyway; the two officers passed her without comment. Loughty turned to the officer who was guarding the body and asked, 'Has a doctor seen the body yet?'

'Oh, umm, not yet,' said the police officer.

He looked like he should have retired some years earlier. But manpower was in short supply after the war. 'When are they due?' asked Loughty.

'Due? Well, ah, yes, you see, I....' started the officer.

'You've not requested one?' said Loughty.

'No, sorry sir.'

'Well go get one, now!' shouted Loughty.

The officer rushed off as fast as his creaky bones allowed. Loughty turned to Humblecut and shrugged. It was not in Loughtys' nature to get dirty, so, as usual, he said, 'Humble, check if the deceased has any obvious wounds? Might as well make a start while we wait. Go through his pockets as well.'

This was before the days of forensics. Humble reluctantly knelt down in the mud and grime of the alley to check the things his boss had asked. Hilda had been examining a distant part of the alley. She walked over just as Loughty spoke to Humble and said, 'You'll find the body has a single pointed entry wound. There's nothing in his pockets. Not even a present.'

Loughty glanced up at Hilda. She was a wraith-like figure in the fog and he asked, 'Who are you?'

'I'm Mrs Hilda Shilton.'

It was hard to see her in detail. Loughty asked her, 'You're not one of these new fangled female medics are you? The wars got a lot to answer for. Bad enough that you left your homes and worked in factories.'

'My, my,' said Hilda. 'You have some strong and unwelcome opinions.'

'Are you the doctor?' asked Loughty.

He was impatient with having to ask again. 'No, but that would be a wheeze,' said Hilda. She then shouted up the alley. 'Pearl, this Scotland Yard chappy thinks I'm a doctor.' Then she said to Loughty, 'No, never was much good at school. Although I am good at detecting.'

'Get this, this woman...' started Loughty. Then as Hilda walked closer and Loughty saw how young she was, he said, 'This girl, out of here Humble.'

'My name is Mrs Hilda Shilton.'

'What?' said Loughty.

'I told you my name earlier and you forgot it,' said Hilda. 'Not very impressive for a detective.'

'I don't care what your name is,' said Loughty. 'Humble, what are you still doing down there? Get her out of here.'

Humble struggled to his feet, brushed the mud from his trousers and said to Hilda, 'If you could please come this way young lady.'

'Mrs Shilton, have you got a poor memory too?'

'Miss I mean Mrs Shilton,' said Humblecut. 'Could you please come with me.'

'No, I couldn't,' said Hilda. 'You shouldn't let him boss you around like that, he's very rude, isn't he?'

'But he's my boss miss...' Hilda stared at him. 'I mean Mrs Shilton, please,' said Humble. Glancing at the floor.

'Now look here...' started Loughty.

'You look here,' said Hilda. 'You get your poor humble servant to kneel in the mud. While you lord it over him. What a fine how do you do.'

Loughty stood, mouth wide, staring at Hilda. Humble said, 'The chief inspector is a great man you know. This is Chief Inspector Loughty of the Yard.'

'Never heard of him,' said Hilda. She turned to Loughty and asked, 'If you're such a great man. Have you solved any big crimes I might have heard of or read about?'

The chief inspector looked flabbergasted. No one had ever challenged him or put him on the spot like this before. He said, 'Well, umm, there was that...' Then he stopped and stared at the floor. After a moment he said, 'Humble, name my biggest cases.'

'Oh, yes, well,' said Sergeant Humblecut, 'It's always difficult isn't it, when you have to come up with things just like that.' He took off his hat and scratched his bald head. 'Now I remember.' He replaced his hat and nodded sagely before continuing, 'There was the famous case of the missing gloves.'

'The case of the missing gloves?' said Hilda. She laughed and shouted to Pearl, 'You need to come and hear this. The Chief Inspector's biggest case was saving a pair of gloves.'

Pearl shouted, 'What's that?'

She then walked up the alley to join everyone by the body. When Pearl arrived, Hilda said, 'Chief Inspector drafty I think his name is.'

'Loughty,' said Humble.

'That's right, laughy here, his biggest case was stopping ladies gloves running away,' said Hilda. 'I suppose he's also an expert in haberdashery.'

'Come on now Mrs Shilton,' said Humble. 'I was saying that Chief Inspector Loughty of the Yard solved the famous case of the missing gloves.'

'I lost a pair of wooly gloves,' said Pearl. 'Can you find those for me?'

'Now look here, you two. Stop making jokes. That was not my biggest case and the sergeant here knows that,' said Loughty, glaring at Humble. 'I have had lots of much bigger cases. I just can't think of them at the moment. But that was an important case, it involved some very important people.'

'The king was it?' asked Hilda.

'No it wasn't His Majesty the King,' it seemed like Loughty was bowing. 'But it was a lady of noble birth,' said Loughty.

'I'm sure she was very glad to have you on the case,' said Hilda. 'Does she call you whenever she misplaces her sundries or smalls. A fine lady must appreciate having a detective keeping track of her personals?'

'I'll have you know that I'm a very important man at the yard,' said Loughty.

'That's good to hear,' said Hilda. 'I'm sure you have a good broom to sweep it with.'

'Hilda, honestly,' said Pearl. Then turning to the chief inspector, she said, 'I apologise for Hilda's odd sense of humour.'

'Indeed,' said Loughty.

He drew himself up to his full height and towered above them all, like an ogre. Hilda ignored the inspectors posturing and said, 'Well, while your trying to remember about the time you saved a pair of slippers that ran away. You may like to know that I am the famous Mrs Hilda Shilton. I solved the murder of a young man in Kilburn when I was just fourteen, didn't I Pearl.' Hilda bowed.

'She did, yes,' said Pearl. 'Although, I'm not sure that makes you famous...'

'Never mind that,' said Hilda, cutting Pearl off. 'I also solved the case of the falling man.'

'Get these two away from here,' shouted Loughty.

Humble accompanied Hilda and Pearl from the scene. Hilda shouted over her shoulder, 'You may be looking for a stiletto type weapon.'

'What!?' said Loughty.

But Hilda and Pearl were already gone. Loughty said out loud, 'A stiletto; of course, why didn't I think of that.'

Humble returned from removing Hilda and Pearl. He asked, 'What's that sir?'

'Nothing,' said Loughty. 'Where's that doctor?'

Chapter Four

That night

Hilda's home, Kilburn, London, UK

As a man in the 1940s; one thing you could always rely on was that your wife would be at home while you were out working. Meaning that a meal would await your return home. Ah, domestic bliss. Or was it? Life is never quite how we expect. Certainly not the way it's shown in movies, books, and magazines. In fiction about the 1940s, they present scenes of marital harmony. But real life was never that way. Spending a day at home doing the housework without a washing machine or modern vacuum cleaners. Cooking without a microwave or convenience food. That wasn't domestic bliss for the women; whatever the men thought. Hilda certainly had no plans to be a slave to domestic drudgery. Arthur didn't see her as his slave. In Hilda's eyes, being freed from work meant being free to pursue her own plans. She'd fit in a bit of simple cooking; most nights. Oh yes, and flick a duster around. As for laundry, that's something Arthur gained an increasing familiarity with over their married life. Equality of the sexes had a head start in the Shilton family.

***

Arthur Shilton worked in Whitehall. Such a boring-looking office from the outside. Yet within the walls of a discrete building lurked spies. Well, maybe not spies, but agents of his majesty's government tasked with intelligence operations... ok, spies. Come to think of it, lurked may not be the right expression. But they certainly worked in the building. The Secret Intelligence Service (SIS) later called MI6, occupied many offices within that rather boring stone edifice.

If you were to wander in and gained access past the retired army sergeant who guarded the door (He appeared to be just another doorman), then you would feel disappointed. Once you had gained entrance, no mean feat in itself, the hallways were long and dark. The offices rang with the sound of typewriters; just like every other office in London at the time. The intelligence agents, when they were in, sat together in a large office. Oddly, considering it housed secret operatives, it had large windows. They never drew the curtains during the day. When you were lucky enough to see a gathering of intelligence agents; a spy ring, perhaps? They dressed like any other businessmen. The only rings were on their fingers and none had any poison darts attached. They actually kept special equipment, like guns and wirelesses, at a remote location. Exciting electronic gadgets wouldn't come till later years. There were several agents who worked every day on intelligence gathering and interpretation. Arthur came into this category. Hilda didn't know about Arthur's actual job. She thought he worked as a civil servant in the War Office. Which, in a way, he did. It's just that he was an intelligence agent.

Every night at five o'clock, Arthur left his office. He had a brisk ten-minute walk to the Embankment Underground Station, commonly called the tube. There he boarded a train on the Bakerloo Line and eleven stops or twenty minutes later, he arrived at Kilburn Park underground station. It was then another brisk ten-minute walk home. We'll ignore the rain that often accompanied those walks. Arthur had a gabardine coat to fend off those showers. Hilda bought it as a wedding gift. A practical rather than fun gift; most unlike her. In this case, it was her pops who suggested it. Arthur already owned the Trilby hat he always wore. Its wide brim, a useful shelter from the regular rainfall. He certainly looked like a spy; the ones in the movies, anyway.

On the night that Hilda had popped into the city and found a dead Father Christmas, Arthur arrived home at his usual time, around six o'clock. It never varied much, as the underground trains ran every few minutes and Arthur always finished on time. As Arthur walked into their home, there was no smell of cooking; nor a smell of burning. That was not uncommon either. Arthur never knew what to expect from his wife. But usually she would at least be home; she attempted to get back for six each night. Often his arrival would prompt her to start dinner preparations; with his help. The normal routine often ran:

Hilda would be sitting reading the local newspaper searching for details on murders or puzzling mysteries. The door would open and she'd leap up and say, 'Is that the time?'

'Hello love,' Arthur would say. 'I suppose dinner isn't started yet?'

Hilda would run over and kiss him, saying, 'It'll just be a jiffy.'

By the time Arthur had changed out of his work suit and put on a comfortable cardigan over his shirt and tie, Hilda would be in the kitchen. He'd walk in and find her dancing around and singing. 'Can I help?' he'd ask.

Hilda would then stop and say, 'I'm glad you're here. Do you want bangers and mash or.... umm.'

'Bangers and mash is fine,' he'd say.

But on arriving that evening, the kitchen was in darkness, as was the entire house. Hilda wasn't sitting at the dining table studying the newspapers, looking for mysteries to solve. No sound of her singing, nor any dancing. Arthur tried shouting Hilda's name, but no answer. He was worried; this was strange, even for Hilda and her unreliable behaviour. Since they had been married two years earlier, she had almost always been there when he returned home. Twice she had been missing. But both times she had told him to expect it. Once she had been out with Pearl shopping. The other time, she was visiting an aunt. Arthur didn't expect to arrive and find a meal on the table. On the occasions when Hilda had forgotten to shop, they had popped out for fish and chips. A few times Arthur had cooked; his mother taught him. Unheard of among his male colleagues. But he expected to find his wife at home. Or at least to have mentioned she'd be out. For Hilda to be totally missing from the house with no warning or note; that was a worry. Arthur stood in the empty kitchen and wondered, 'Where was she?'

Arthur was a man of action; well he was a spy. Isn't that in the job description? It's true that he only worked in an office - for now. But he knew what to do. He headed out of the house and down the road. At last, another advantage to living around the corner from Hilda's parents. She may be visiting her mother; unlikely, but possible. At least she may know where Hilda had gone. That was where Hilda had been on one occasion she had been missing. Picking up a box from her parents' attic. Something urgent she needed. But this time, as Arthur stood on Hilda's parent's doorstep, it seemed less promising. After a few knocks, Hilda's mother, Henrietta, answered the door. She acted oddly and didn't invite him in. A male voice called from inside, 'Who's at the door?'

The male voice didn't sound like Hilda's father. Besides, he shouldn't be home. Arthur worked with Bert, Hilda's father, at SIS. So Arthur knew Bert was away on a top secret mission for the week.

Henrietta ignored the male voice as if it had not spoken. She assured Arthur she didn't know where Hilda could be. Arthur stood outside and planned his next move. The curtains of Hilda's parents' house twitched. A man peeked out. It looked like their neighbour, Sid. That couldn't be right. Arthur decided he must be imagining it with all the stress of searching for Hilda. The mind can play tricks under duress. That was one of the things they taught him on a training course for spies he attended in Scotland. Arthur was being prepared to work as a field agent. That needed lots of preparation. Part of that involved survival training on his own up a cold and wet mountain in the highlands of Scotland. The man running the course had trained them well. One thing he had drummed into the agents on the course was, 'When you're under stress, your mind will play tricks.'

Arthur decided Sid couldn't be standing at Hilda's parents' house peeping out from behind the curtains. So Arthur said to himself, 'It's just your anxious mind playing tricks; pull yourself together.'

After standing for a few minutes by Hilda's parents' house, being watched by an imaginary Sid, or maybe the real Sid. After all, Hilda had often noted that the real, not an imaginary Sid often visited her mother when her pops was away. Henrietta had a guilty secret; maybe this was it. But Arthur knew nothing of this and carried on, searching. The figure at the window closed the curtains – or maybe the curtains closed on their own. Let's not get caught up in Arthur's stress based imaginings.

As Arthur walked away from Hilda's parents' house and the real or imaginary Sid, it occurred to him that Hilda may be with her best friend, Pearl. If he knew one thing, it was that Hilda spent a lot of time with her best friend. In fact, whenever the weekend came around and he was free to be with his wife; she popped off with her best friend Pearl. It's a surprise he didn't go there first. Arthur headed to Pearl's house, or rather Pearl's parent's, where she still lived. As he walked along, Arthur thought about how married life was not all he expected.

On arrival at the house, Pearl's mother, Eileen, answered the door and said, 'Hello, Arthur, I bet you've been wondering where your wife is. I told her it was time to go. But you know your Hilda.'

'Not as well as I thought,' said Arthur. 'Thank goodness she's here.'

'They're upstairs,' said Eileen. 'Come in and join the party.'

Arthur's tummy rumbled with hunger. Perhaps the word party had triggered it. Or maybe it was just that his dinner was overdue. Eileen sent Arthur upstairs. As he ascended the stairs, he felt awkward heading to Pearl's bedroom. So he called ahead, saying, 'It's just me, Arthur.'

Gentlemen didn't enter young ladies' bedrooms uninvited in the 1940s; not well-bred gentlemen like Arthur. As he drew near the door, Hilda spotted him and said, 'Oh hello. Is that the time already, come in. Pearl got carried away with everything.'

'What!?' said Pearl. 'I got carried away.'

'You see,' said Hilda. 'Glad you admitted it.'

As Arthur entered Pearl's bedroom, he stood and gazed in awe. The wall had newspaper cuttings stuck all over it and there were other notes all over the bed. 'What's all this?' he asked.

'Pearl and I found Father Christmas dead,' said Hilda. 'Not the real one, of course. He'll be busy at the North Pole getting all my presents ready. Anyway, Scotland Yard have sent Lanky.'

'Loughty,' said Pearl.

'That's the one and Humblechops,' said Hilda.

'Humblecut,' said Pearl.

'As I said. Leggy and Bumble, neither of them had ever solved more than some runaway smalls. So I thought we'd better get involved,' said Hilda. 'They need a proper professional detective.'

Arthur and Pearl both shook their heads and stared at Hilda, wide eyed.

The Next Day

Scotland Yard, London, UK

The two officers who Hilda had derided were sitting in Chief Inspector Loughty's office the next afternoon. Humblecut had just handed his boss the preliminary medical report. Not that the detailed one would have much more information. This was 1948 after all. Loughty read it and said, ' Listen to this Humble, The sawbones says: "Victim had high levels of alcohol and signs of long-term use." That probably applies to most men who take that job. I mean, who'd want to be a Father Christmas? Here's a great bit: "The body was dirty and unkempt, worn and dirty fingernails," he didn't he see the state of that alley. Oh, here we go, I see that the doctor agrees with me. "A stiletto type weapon is the most likely to have inflicted the fatal wound." That's the only bit we need.'

'Oh, right, yes sir,' said Humblecut, raising an eyebrow. Perhaps he remembered Hilda's passing comment as she left. 'I did read it. What's your thinking on that sir?'

'Italian's,' said Loughty.

'Sorry sir, I'm not clear on your meaning?'

'The Italians are guilty,' said Loughty.

'All of them?' asked Humblecut.

'Quite possibly Humble, I never liked Italian's or Italy for that matter.'

'That's a bit sweeping isn't it sir.'

'They were very quick to join Herr Hitler and just and fast to drop him,' said Loughty.

To say that Loughty was a bigoted and narrow-minded man would be to give bigots and narrow-minded people a bad name. Few, if anybody, were as narrowminded as Loughty. Humblecut stared at his boss in horror and said, 'But sir, isn't it more likely that only one man committed these murders?'

'True,' said Loughty. 'How to narrow it down, that's the thing. Maybe we should round up all the Italians in central London, bang them all up in jail and question them one by one. See who looks guilty and keep that one for the magistrate. That's always worked for me in the past.'

Humblecut grimaced, perhaps remembering previous cases. Then said, 'I think rounding up every Italian in London would cause a major problem. I'm not sure we have enough cells. The commissioner may not be happy either.'

'Really?' said Loughty, looking puzzled. 'Maybe you're right. It would take a lot of my time and my time is valuable.'

'Yes, quite,' said Humblecut. 'I was wondering if we should revisit the scene of the crime today. Now the fogs lifted.'

'No need for that,' said Loughty. 'We know it's the same murderer and that dank alley won't have changed since last night. We'd do better spending our time checking out local Italian villains. That's the key to all this. If we can't bring them all in, we can at least question the real rogues. Narrow it down. Perhaps we can start at that little Italian Bistro we like.'

'Do you think the criminal is hiding at Cafe Bella?' asked Humblecut.

'Of course not,' said Loughty. 'I've not had lunch yet and we can probably assume our favourite restaurant owner is innocent.'

Perhaps we should leave Loughty while he fills his stomach and pursues his... maybe leads is too strong a word for them.

Alley by Carvey Michaels, London, UK

While Chief Inspector Loughty was denigrating the whole of Italy and indeed the whole Italian population of London, Hilda was back at the scene of the crime. She had in mind trying to find the actual murderer. Which is quite a good idea in a murder investigation. Maybe Loughty could learn a thing or two from her. Hilda didn't focus on racial profiling. Not that she or Loughty would understand that concept. It was many years from being introduced. No doubt Humblecut would have preferred to be with Hilda than his boss. But he lacked the courage to cross the chief inspector.

In the alley, the fog had lifted, giving Hilda a much better view. Let's hope that the fog will soon lift on the Scotland Yard investigation. Without the existence of plastic tape or a forensic investigation, the only evidence of a murder in the alley next to the Carvey Michael's store was the bloodstain on the concrete. Hilda stood staring at the stain for a considerable length of time. Not because she had a particular interest in blood stains per se; but because you can learn a lot from a bloodstain. At least that's what she had recently read in a murder mystery called, 'Blood on the Carpet.' Hilda had been binge reading lots of detective novels. In that novel, the detective had solved the murder by the shape of the bloodstain. As Hilda stared at the bloodstain on the concrete, she decided this murder would not be solved the same way. But Hilda remained convinced that she could learn how to be a brilliant detective from fictional novels. Who needed facts when you had fiction? If it wasn't for the great love she had of her woollen bonnet, Hilda would wear a deerstalker like Sherlock Holmes. She had tried smoking a pipe; but soon gave up. Such a filthy habit. The only thing she used from that famous fictional detective was a magnifying glass. This essential piece of detecting equipment was up to her eye at that very moment. Hilda couldn't understand why it made everything blurry. She then tried getting closer to the ground, and the bloodstain became sharp. 'That's better,' she said out loud.

'What is dear lady?' asked a man.

He was sitting in a recess set within the wall a short way up from where the Father Christmas had been murdered. Hilda looked up at the stranger and asked, 'Who are you?'

He was very blurry until Hilda removed the magnifying glass from her eye. The stranger looked at Hilda and said, 'I might ask the same question young lady.'

'I am the world famous detective, Mrs Hilda Shilton.'

The man stood up in respect for someone so famous. He bowed, walked forward, took Hilda's hand and said, 'I'm honoured to meet you. Although, I'm ashamed to say I've not heard of you before.'

'That's quite alright,' said Hilda. 'We can't all be perfect.'

'Thank you for your gracious understanding,' said the man. 'The mark of a true gentlewoman.'

'How kind. But what's your name?' asked Hilda.

'The Marquess of Messex at your service.'

He bowed again, more deeply this time. Hilda looked puzzled and asked, 'A Marquess? Aren't they tents?'

'A marquee is a kind of tent,' said The Marquess of Messex.

'That's what I said.'

'They are spelt differently, but sound the same,' said the marquess.

'How very confusing,' said Hilda. 'I hope no one tries to shelter under you?'

'As you can see, they would be out of luck my dear lady. I am rather on my uppers,' said the marquess.

He waved towards his limited shelter in the dark recess of the wall. Hilda walked over to it, glanced down at the few tatty blankets and asked, 'You're living here? In this alley?'

'It is my unfortunate situation,' said the marquess.

Hilda asked, 'I don't suppose you were at home when this happened?'

She pointed at the bloodstain. The marquess said, 'Alas, seldom do I get invited to many functions anymore.'

'In that case, I have some questions for you,' said Hilda.

'I will endeavour to serve as best I can.'

Hilda came away with some interesting extra information. Things that Scotland Yard should really have found out. Indeed, had Humblecut been in charge, they would have discovered them.

Hilda's home, Kilburn, London, UK

The next Sunday, after lunch, Arthur was sitting reading the Times newspaper. This was a particular indulgence of his and one he struggled to enjoy in peace. Hilda had a tendency to either put on the wireless in the afternoon for a bit of music. She enjoyed dancing and singing around the house. Or, if Arthur convinced his wife that a quiet afternoon was in order, she would find a hobby to sit and enjoy. The only problem was that Hilda did no hobby quietly. She decided to try out knitting; a new thing for her. Hilda's mother had given up trying to teach her and the teacher at Miss Wentworth's Academy for Young Ladies decided Hilda was a lost cause on knitting, cooking and sewing. Cooking being the strangest one. Considering Hilda later becoming head cook at the BBC. Hilda had wondered about returning to Miss Wentworths and boasting of that fact after she attained that lofty position. But, perhaps it's as well she didn't.

On that Sunday afternoon, Hilda sat with her knitting and said out loud, 'Now, I seem to remember that Pearl's name came into this.'

Arthur glanced up from his newspaper and said, 'Could you please work it out in your head, my love?'

'Of course dearest,' said Hilda. 'I just needed to check a few little things. As a civil servant you must know what it's like? All those tiny details?'

'Yes I do, thank you.'

Arthur picked his paper back up and continued reading. Hilda huffed and puffed. Held the pattern close and far away. Then decided it must be upside down. She shook her head and turned it back the other way. Eventually, she picked up the knitting needles and tried to work out how to hold them. After a few attempts and picking them up three times; she wrapped some wool around the needles and she was off. At first she whispered, 'Knit one, Pearl one.'

But Arthur looked up, and she stopped. Her mouth moved, but no words came out. She carried on mouthing the words for ten minutes, then held up her knitting to admire it. The few loops of wool she had managed to get onto her needles all fell off. She captured none of them into a knitted form. 'Bother,' she said.

Hilda got up and went off to make a cup of tea. At least she knew how to make that. It had been high on her list of things to learn after they were married. Arthur had assumed that because Hilda was head chef at the BBC, Hilda would be a wonderful cook. He was unaware that she had rather smooth talked her way into that job and relied on good luck and the help of her staff to survive there.

Arthur had progressed a fair way through his paper when Hilda wheeled a trolley through. It had a pot of tea and some bread and jam. It was their Sunday afternoon treat. Rationing meant that food treats were few and far between. As Hilda appeared Arthur said, 'Wasn't that Scotland Yard chappie you met called Loughty?'

'Either that or Shifty,' said Hilda. 'Mind you he was tall, so maybe it was Lofty.' She sorted the tea out.

'Well, he's in The Times. Famous chap.'

'He was a bit full of himself,' said Hilda, buttering the bread thinly.

'Apparently he recovered a Lady V's gloves.'

Hilda looked at her husband quizzically and asked, 'Lady V? Who's that?'

Arthur glanced at his wife and said, 'The Times is rather circumspect with the aristocracy. Giving them the benefit of privacy.'

Hilda shrugged and said, 'Well, I never. Laughing boy did mention some fine lady and her lost gloves. So his man Shambles was right.'

'Do you want me to read the story?' asked Arthur.

'Let me pour the tea and finish spreading the jam and then you can.'

Chapter Five

End of December 1948

Hilda's home, Kilburn, London, UK

Newspapers give such abbreviated and sensationalised versions of events. After all, they want to sell papers and the reporters weren't present at the time. So a little artistic licence is forgivable. But had Arthur and Hilda been able to go back to the events articled in *The Times* that Sunday morning, this is what they would have seen and heard:

Two Years Earlier, December 1946

Wold Castle, North East, UK

Winter 1946 was the coldest for many years. Snow had been falling continuously and by December, many roads were impassible. We all like a white Christmas, but there are limits even for a chionophile. That's someone who loves the snow and cold weather. Hilda found that word on one of her regular trips to the local library. She stored it away in her brain, ready to forget; she never did very well at remembering words. Most of us are not chionophiles; a few inches of snow and a slight drop in temperature will do very nicely, thank you. But weeks and weeks of arctic weather is no fun at all. For the people living in Great Britain still suffering the privations of war; rationing, poor housing, and lack of fuel, the conditions in the winter of 1946 were extremely unwelcome.

At Wold Castle, Lord, and Lady Vernon had an advantage over many others. Wealth and their own sources of food and fuel. Every day, they dispatched their few remaining staff into their forest to gather firewood. Well, you can't expect her ladyship to hoick up her skirts and gather kindling; that wouldn't be seemly. No matter how liberal minded a member of the aristocracy she was, and she certainly came into that classification; but there are limits.

Unusual; would be an excellent description of Lady Virginia Vernon. Or maybe we could call her an example of virtue and charity. Whatever we call her, she was not typical of her class at the time. Many of them gave to charity both their time and money. Few were quite as giving in nature as Lady Vernon. In her eyes, the tenants living on the Wold Castle estate mattered as people. They had value as fellow human beings. One might think that's obvious; but you'd be looking at things through modern eyes. The aristocracy at the time saw their staff and tenants more as a responsibility or something they owned. Lady Vernon was a woman ahead of her time. She noted how cold and bleak the weather had become and gathered many of the tenants into Wold Castle itself; her home. Those who were unable to heat their homes took priority. Having taken this extraordinary step; she then limited the number of rooms that the Vernon family themselves used and heated. Most amazing was her act of sharing the Vernon family's own food with the estate families. Not just those she gathered within her walls; but also those remaining within their own homes.

Lord John Veron saw his wife's actions as the beginning of the end of English life. He felt the madness in eastern Europe had influenced her; and expected a full revolution in England to follow. But he could never refuse his wife anything. As the days of freezing winter stretched into weeks and then into months, everyone wondered how long they could all last. The Vernon food supplies were not limitless.

***

A couple of weeks into their strange new life at Wold Castle, a problem arose. One not related to a shortage of food or fuel. Lord and Lady Vernon needed to call in outside help. Lady Vernon convinced her husband that the detecting skills of Scotland Yard were required. In truth, the order of things had been:

Lady Vernon stood in front of her husband's desk. He was barely visible over the piles of papers. She said, 'We need to call in PC Riley.'

Lord Vernon had stared at his wife between the piles of papers. It was bad enough she had interrupted his morning newspaper reading. After coughing in annoyance, he said, 'Riley can just about cope with finding a missing cat.'

'Who do you suggest we call?' asked Lady Vernon.

'I have an old army friend,' said Lord Vernon. 'He's commissioner at Scotland Yard. I'm sure he'll sort something out.'

'So long as he does,' said Lady Vernon. 'This is a very important matter, I hope you'll handle it forthwith.'

She was about to leave when her husband said, 'Ah, now about that.'

He then involved her in sending the telegram. He hated such new-fangled ideas as telegrams.

Scotland Yard, London, UK

The Commissioner of Scotland Yard sat staring at the telegram from his friend, Lord Vernon. In reality, from Lady Vernon. The commissioner smiled and said to himself, 'I know just the man for this job.'

Recently, he'd been hearing complaints from junior officers that Chief Inspector Loughty was not performing well. This case would both test that out and send Loughty on a cold trip north. The commissioner had not appreciated Loughty's recent comments at a public meeting. Comments that had made the commissioner look foolish. He didn't like to be made a fool of by his staff. But Loughty was a hard man to discipline directly. A bit of fear came into the situation. The commissioner needed an excuse to simply send the man a letter or have a junior officer handle the situation.

Whether or not the reports were accurate, Loughty needed taking down a peg or two. The commissioner smirked as he handed the telegram to an officer to pass on to Loughty's sergeant.

***

A short while later Chief Inspector later sat staring at his sergeant. Humblecut had just read the telegram out loud. Loughty asked, 'They want us to go where?'

Sergeant Humblecut took a step back from his chief's desk. He glanced back at the telegram and said, 'Sorry sir, I don't recognise it. Wold Castle.'

'Oh, I do. It's a godforsaken place up in the north east,' said Loughty. 'Isn't it cold enough here?

Humblecut glanced at the blazing fire in his chief's office. The sergeant shared a general office and one fire with a staff of six. He shuffled sideways towards the fire and said, 'Right, I see sir.'

'How on earth will we get there?' asked Loughty.

'I think the train is running,' said Humblecut. 'They have snow ploughs I believe.'

Loughty snorted, then he smiled and said, 'I suppose the commissioner wanted to send his best man eh Humble?'

Humble nodded and turned his back towards the fire, hands warming nicely. Loughty rose and the two men headed out of the office.

Wold Castle, North East, UK

Lady Vernon had taken to having her breakfast in bed. It was fast becoming the warmest place in their home. Her staff had moved her bed nearer to the fireplace. She stayed there till late morning and then joined the newly extended household for luncheon. This morning, she had a telegram on her breakfast tray. As Lord Vernon had insisted, she send the telegram; he also insisted she deal with the reply. Thus, even though it was addressed to him, he sent it up to her.

Lord Vernon still rose as usual and ate breakfast in his study. He gave orders not to be disturbed for any reason. He had reinforced that order after his wife disturbed him the previous day to discuss involving the police in their little problem. There were rumours about why he may want privacy. That perhaps he received an occasional visitor. But no one confirmed such scandalous comments. After all, the rumour suggested the visitor was a young woman.

Lady Vernon's maid, Betty, brought the telegram on the breakfast tray. 'There's a telegram for you m'lady,' said Betty. 'Well, for his Lordship really...'

'I understand, thank you Betty, can you get my warmest clothes ready for later. I think I should make an appearance; eventually.' Lady Vernon smiled.

Betty nodded and headed over to the wardrobe to prepare the relevant attire.

Lady Vernon read the telegram:

From: Commissioner Davidson STOP
To: Verny STOP

Have sent best man STOP
Arrive on the noon train. STOP
Should solve problem. STOP
Danky STOP

'Stupid nicknames,' said Lady Vernon.
'What's that, my lady?' asked Betty.
Her head was partway in the large wardrobe. 'My husband and his wartime friends that's all. Danky, Tinpot, and Balaclava Bert. Don't you go sharing that with the other staff.'
'Never my lady,' said Betty.
The maid popped her head around the wardrobe door and smiled. Lady Vernon said, 'Looks like we have visitors arriving. A bigwig from Scotland Yard and no doubt he'll have a junior officer with him.'
'I'll tell the housekeeper m'lady.'

***

Next morning, Chief Inspector Loughty and Sergeant Humblecut sat alone in the dining room at Wold Castle. They were pointlessly waiting for breakfast. No one had told them about the new household arrangements. Lady Vernon took breakfast in bed as usual. His Lordship partook in his study, maybe alone. Those tenants lucky enough to have gained rooms at Wold Castle ate with the servants. The household staff had reduced over the years since the two wars. So there was plenty of room in the staff dining room. It was also one of the warmest places in the house.

After waiting fifteen minutes, Loughty said, 'Right Humble, go and find out what the hold up is.'

'Oh, umm, will do,' said Humblecut.

He reluctantly headed off in search of the staff. Meanwhile, Loughty found an old newspaper, sat back and read.

***

In the servants' dining room, breakfast was a raucous affair these days. When the old butler had died, Lord Vernon had struggled to find a suitable replacement. The senior footman, James, stepped up. At twenty-two, he had barely enough experience. But Lord Vernon had no other options. James acted as the perfect butler in the presence of His Lordship. He also came to an arrangement with the staff that they played their part; when on show. That way, his lordship felt that all was well. But, below stairs, life differed greatly from before. Thus, breakfast was a time of laughter and bawdy humour. The like of which must have caused the previous butler to spin in his grave.

Humblecut walked in and stood for a few minutes, trying to gain attention. In the end, he had to do something quite out of character. He coughed, no effect, and then shouted, 'Excuse me.'

James looked up at the interloper from his place at the head of the table and said, 'You're excused, Mr Humblecut.' Gales of laughter ensued around the table. Then James said, 'Do take a seat. Is your chief still asleep?'

'Well, no actually, he err, well we were waiting,' said Humblecut.

He pointed upstairs. The laughter was even louder than before. Once it settled down, the cook said, 'You poor dear, did no one tell ee? We eat down 'ere in the morn.'

Humblecut blushed and said quietly, 'That explains it. I'll go and tell the chief inspector.'

'Don't you put yourself to any trouble,' said James, 'and don't stand on ceremony, sit down and tuck in. I'll send a lad up to get him.'

'If you're sure,' said Humblecut.

James gave Humblecut a seat next to him. After eating for about ten minutes. Humblecut realised Loughty had not arrived. He turned to James and said, 'I think your lad may have got lost.'

'I'd forget my head,' said James. 'Davy, pop upstairs and tell that gentleman where breakfast is.'

Humblecut stared in horror at James. When Loughty arrived a few minutes later, Humblecut tried to avoid looking at him. Though the chief seemed a lot happier after he'd eaten.

***

Later that morning, Lady Vernon held an audience with the two detectives in a small sitting room. She reclined on a sofa in front of a blazing fire. The days of entertaining guests in the larger rooms would have to wait. A tray of tea was before her, but it lacked the usual plate of cakes or other fancies. Lady Vernon told the detectives to sit and poured the tea. Then she said, 'What do you know about my missing gloves?'

'Assume we know nothing,' said Loughty.

He always used that line, and in this case, it was more accurate than usual. Lady Vernon nodded, sipped her tea, then put her cup down and sat back. 'I need to take you back a few months,' she said. 'The Earl of Hurlington visited. You may or may not know. He's our son-in-law, married our eldest daughter ten years ago. Sadly, she died in childbirth a year after their marriage. He brought our grandson, Lord Edward, with him. We see our grandson so seldom these days, it was a great joy to see him.'

Lady Vernon smiled sadly and picked up her tea again. She sipped it slowly. Loughty asked, 'Was that when your gloves were stolen?'

'No, not at all,' said Lady Vernon, replacing her teacup on its saucer; daintily. 'I am telling you this because on that visit the earl told us something shocking.'

Loughty and Humblecut sat forward expectantly. Lady Vernon stared off towards a picture on the wall. It was a picture of a young lad; her grandson, Lord Edward. Loughty glanced between the picture and Lady Vernon, then said, 'You were saying, that he told you something shocking.'

'Yes he did,' said Lady Vernon. 'Oh, of course. I've not told you what it was. He said...' she stared hard at Loughty and Humblecut and asked, 'This is confidential, can you promise me it won't go any further?'

'That depends your ladyship. If it involves a murder or...' started Loughty.

'Oh nothing like that,' cut in Lady Vernon.

'In that case, we promise,' said Loughty.

He stared at Humblecut, who nodded in agreement. Lady Vernon sighed and said, 'The Earl of Hurlington told us that he was bankrupt, penniless. Poor investments after the war or something. I don't understand these things, I am just a woman after all.' Loughty nodded sagely. Lady Vernon continued, 'He said that his one hope was a treasure his father had left in Barbados. They owned plantations over there you know. It's where their wealth came from. His father had buried some gold for a rainy day and kept a hidden a map for it.'

'That sounds hopeful,' said Humblecut. Speaking for the first time.

Lady Vernon looked at the sergeant in surprise. Then said, 'It would have been, only the earl didn't know where this map was.'

'I see,' said Humblecut.

'Where do your gloves come into all this?' asked Loughty.

'Just be patient,' said Lady Vernon. 'We didn't hear from the earl after that for quite a long time. His Lordship read in The Times all about the bankruptcy. So embarrassing for the family, of course.'

'So it's not a secret,' said Humblecut under his breath.

Lady Vernon appeared not to hear the sergeant. She said, 'Then, a couple of weeks ago, the earl arrived on his own, unannounced, late at night. I have no idea how he made it through such deep snow. It freezes so hard you know.'

'Yes, it's hard enough in the daytime,' said Loughty.

Humblecut nodded. Lady Vernon continued, 'The earl was in a strange mood. He looked haggard and drawn. Like he hadn't slept in a week. He kept asking about the gloves they'd given to me as a gift on their wedding day.'

'The gloves at last,' said Loughty.

'No need to be impatient chief inspector,' said Lady Vernon. 'That's right. These were the gloves. They gave them to me as a thankyou for all I did to help with the wedding. He said they were a family heirloom.'

'Why give you a tatty old pair of gloves?' asked Loughty.

'They weren't tatty,' said Lady Vernon. Staring at the chief inspector in horror. 'The workmanship was exquisite. They were made by the finest glove makers in Europe.'

'Did he explain why he needed them?' asked Humblecut.

'No, he didn't say,' said Lady Vernon. 'But I agreed to have them fetched down for him forthwith. However, Betty, my maid, couldn't find them. Then the earl acted very strangely. He wouldn't believe my maid. Indeed he went completely crazy. I felt quite faint. He was so angry. Throwing things around and shouting. He grabbed Betty and nearly throttled her.' Lady Vernon wafted herself with her hand and breathed deeply.

'It's alright Lady Vernon, you take your time,' said Humblecut.

'Yes, it's all a bit much for a woman,' said Loughty.

'I must say, that I had never seen such violence,' said Lady Vernon. 'He ranted and raved, accusing Betty of stealing the gloves. I had to call James to keep him from... well anyway. By the time James arrived the earl had run out into the freezing night, still shouting.'

Lady Vernon sat back, sighing. 'Why on earth would he want your gloves?' said Loughty.

'I have no clue,' said Lady Vernon. 'That's what's so strange about all this. They were a beautiful pair of gloves. But hardly worth enough to rescue them, financially I mean if sold. Not that I could imagine the earl asking for a gift to be returned. But then before that night I couldn't imagine him acting the way he did.'

Humblecut had been nodding and scratching his chin. He asked Lady Vernon, 'What did the gloves look like, the pattern on them?'

'Why on earth does that matter?' asked Loughty. Then, turning to Lady Vernon, he said, 'I apologise for my sergeant. He has some strange ideas.'

'No, that's quite alright. You never know what might be important,' said Lady Vernon. 'They had an interesting pattern inside and out.'

'Would you say it resembled a map?' asked Humblecut. 'Even just slightly?'

'Now that's an interesting idea sergeant,' said Lady Vernon. 'Yes, the embroidery did look a little like a map.'

Loughty snorted and said, 'Right, so the gloves were the missing treasure map. You really do get some very outlandish ideas Humble. The important question is who stole them? Not what they looked like.'

Loughty got up and paced. He wanted to give the impression of thinking. But Lady Vernon was staring at Humblecut. She nodded and had a look on her face that showed the light had dawned.

***

It's just as well that Chief Inspector Loughty of the Yard had Sergeant Humblecut by his side. The term 'unsung hero' springs to mind. Perhaps it's not that surprising that neither officer had been able to rapidly recall any detecting successes for Loughty – he had none to recall. No cases that Loughty had solved alone, that is. Many cases had come across Loughty's desk and many had been solved. Humblecut had solved all of them. But the sergeant lived up to his name and never pushed himself forward; thus, no one realised the truth. Perhaps only his fellow officers. Which was why they kept complaining to the commissioner.

***

That night, Humblecut settled into the drafty guest bedroom that had been assigned to him at Wold Castle. As a lesser employee, his room was in the servants' section and lacked a fire. Presumably, the expectation was for servants to keep warm through hard work. Humblecut pulled the few thin blankets over his head. Trying to think when you are cold is not easy, but he managed it. Earlier that day, Loughty had sent Humblecut around the castle and the estate to investigate. As Loughty said, 'Gather all the clues and bring them to me. I'll then solve the case.'

Loughty had a higher view of his abilities than was justified. Humblecut had started by questioning the staff. He found the cook resting in her room, gin bottle to hand, and caused her to wake abruptly. She shrieked and said, 'Bless me, I thought the divil himself had cum to get me.'

'I'm sorry,' said Humblecut. 'Can I just ask about her Ladyship's gloves?'

'I'd never be stealin notin,' said the cook.

'I'm not accusing you of stealing them,' said Humblecut. 'Did you see anything unusual on the days before the Earl of Hurlington arrived looking for them?'

'Oooo, what a day that was, all a hollerin an a shoutin, I'm a God fearin woman and I had to cover me ears,' said the cook.

'What about in the week or two before he arrived?'

The cook stared at Humblecut, screwed up her face, pursed her lips, then raised her eyebrows and said, 'You mean the gravedigger?'

'Possibly,' said Humblecut.

'Then agin, he mayn't ave bin a gravedigger may he?'

'I don't know? You saw him.'

'Just like he had a spade an all covered in mud.'

'Who was he calling to see?' asked Humblecut.

'It aint me that answers the door. That'd be James. I were just passing. That there gravedigger were at the servants door an rightly so.'

Humblecut went in search of James and asked, 'Who was the gravedigger that called a couple of weeks back?'

'Gravedigger?' asked James. 'Wherever did you get that story from? Oh, don't tell me Molly our cook's been at the gin again.'

'It was the cook,' said Humblecut.

'We haven't had any gravediggers calling at the Castle while I've been butler. But Molly, has a morbid fear of death. Especially when she's hit the bottle. I reckon she wouldn't be here if staff were easier to find.'

'Anyone strange call before the earl turned up looking for his gloves?' asked Humblecut.

'If I were you, I'd be looking closer to home. Know what I mean? His Lordship spends a lot of time *alone* in his study. Except, he isn't exactly alone the whole time, if you see what I'm saying. But you never heard it from me. Not about any female company.'

Acting on that suggestion, Humblecut set himself up in a place with a good view of his Lordship's study door. There he stayed, hidden from view all that afternoon. Other than Lord Vernon and James, no one came or went. He would need to repeat it the next morning.

***

Humblecut forwent breakfast and setup outside Lord Vernon's study from first thing. Cook gave him a hunk of bread and jam to give him sustenance. By late morning, Humblecut was ready to give up. He stood up. The creek of his bones meant he nearly missed the first sound. But the next few steps were more pronounced. The young woman was trying to tiptoe, but failing. She tapped lightly on the study door and must have received an invitation to enter as she disappeared inside. It was after dinnertime before she left.

When Humblecut knocked on the study door, he was also invited to enter. As he walked in, the surprise on Lord Vernon's face suggested he may have assumed his female guest had forgotten something. 'What do you want?' asked Lord Vernon brusquely.

'Sorry my Lord,' said Humblecut. 'I need to ask you an important question.'

'Get on with it man.'

'The woman who just left, did you *lend* her your wife's gloves?'

Lord Vernon's face turned a wonderful shade of puce. He rose to his feet and shouted, 'Get out!'

Humblecut summoned all his courage and said, 'I'm very sorry, my Lord. But this is important. I will tell no one else. You may not have heard from your wife. But those gloves have a treasure map on them that will save your son-in-law and grandson from penury?'

Lord Vernon opened and closed his mouth. It was obvious that Lord Vernon was torn about what to do. Then he said, 'I want your word this doesn't leave this room.'

'Absolutely, I swear on my mothers life,' said Humblecut. 'All I want is to find those gloves.'

'This is what we will do,' said Lord Vernon. 'Tomorrow I will get those gloves back. I admit nothing about where they have been.' Humblecut nodded. Lord Vernon continued, 'Then hand them to you. After that you can arrange to "find" them on a search you make in the grounds.'

'Agreed,' said Humblecut.

***

Next day Lord Vernon did as he had arranged. His lady friend was not happy to lose the beautiful gloves. Lord Vernon was also cross about having to pay for a more beautiful replacement. Humblecut carried out a search of the grounds and "found" the gloves half hidden behind a stone statue. It's just as well that DNA evidence was not around and fingerprints were not possible on the material of the gloves.

Chief Inspector Loughty took all the praise for finding Lady Vernon gloves. Loughty made a great show of returning them to her ladyship. The chief inspector explained that he had worked out where they would be and 'sent his man to retrieve them.'

The Earl of Hurlington used the map hidden on the gloves to find his buried gold and restore his fortune. His mother-in-law, Lady Vernon, being a forgiving woman, said no more about his 'search' for the gloves a few weeks earlier. He was glad to forget that incident. The earl was so happy with Chief Inspector Loughty that he ensured the King awarded him with an honour to thank him. Meanwhile, the true hero, Humblecut, carried on in the background. The Commissioner of Scotland Yard was pleased with the successful resolution of the case. But had to put up with Chief Inspector Loughty boasting about his 'great skills' at solving it. It had not turned out as he planned. The commissioner also had to handle a rather rude letter from his old army mate, Lord Vernon, who complained about the way the case was solved. Verny refused to specify exactly what he meant by that; even when the two men met up at their London club some months later. Verny just touched his nose and said, 'A woman was involved.'

CHAPTER SIX

End of December 1948

Hilda's home, Kilburn, London, UK

Wouldn't it be wonderful if we could see the details of events in such details? But the newspaper only mentioned the known facts of the case of Lady Vernon's missing gloves. The report was brief and to the point; it read as follows:

> Chief Inspector Loughty of Scotland Yard has once again showed the best skills and character of an officer from that fine establishment. The chief inspector was called upon by a certain Lord V. A peer of the realm, to discover the whereabouts of his fine lady's valuable heirloom. That is a fine pair of gloves. It had been discovered that these exquisitely embellished accoutrements held a treasure map.

This map bore the location of a treasure belonging to a close family member, the Earl of H. The location of the treasure had faded from the Earl's family memory. Such a tale brings to mind Treasure Island.

The chief inspector's faithful sergeant accompanied him, as is the tradition of our fine police force. This reporter understands that no members of Lord V's staff were involved in the theft of these gloves. As we expect of those in service to the finest households.

Chief Inspector Loughty said, 'The thief must have taken a fancy to these gloves whilst looking for other items to steal. No doubt he dropped the gloves whilst attempting to escape from the estate. The weather was particularly foul.'

It is our understanding that the Earl of H. may have suffered some minor financial difficulties prior to recovering this map. We believe other, less reputable newspapers have reported the details of such. Indeed, he and his son, Lord E, are currently at a villa in the South of France.

This story is a fine example of to the fact that we can trust in the law of this glorious land and the officers who serve our great and noble King.

After hearing Arthur read the newspaper article, Hilda said, 'Well, if I need to find my gloves I know who to ask.'

'Don't you think putting a treasure map on gloves was a clever idea?' asked Arthur.

'Bit silly if you ask me. I'd have realised they were a map the moment I saw them.'

Arthur shook his head and then, sniffing the air, asked, 'Is that burning I smell?'

'Oops, I forgot to turn off the oven,' said Hilda, running out the door.

SIS, Whitehall, London, UK

On Monday morning, Comander Jameson, the head of SIS, sent Bert to meet a contact from the KGB. It was one of those meetings that no one in government liked to admit happened, but all governments needed in order to keep the wheels moving. The KGB contact was a lowly cipher clerk from the embassy. They were unaware of the importance of their mission. Their boss just gave them a piece of paper and instructions. Jameson could have chosen an equally lowly staff member for the meeting. But he wanted to ensure that all went well.

The two men, Bert, and the cipher clerk, met in a London cafe. Meet is perhaps a strong word. The cipher clerk had a KGB shadow following him. The KGB didn't know about their government's secret meeting, and besides, they didn't trust anyone. Bert, while fairly senior in SIS, was not a field agent and not known to the KGB agent tailing the cipher clerk. A deliberate choice on Jameson's part.

As Bert arrived first, he found a corner seat in the crowded smoky cafe. Other SIS agents, who didn't know the full picture, had set everything up beforehand. The cipher clerk walked in; closely followed by his shadow. The only seats remaining were at Bert's table. He sat next to Bert. The KGB shadow hesitated, then stood near the counter. He watched the clerk closely. Bert continued to stare at his drink and yet spoke quietly to the cipher clerk, 'You'll have a wait for a drink.'

The clerk stared at a poster on the wall. It remained from the war and read, "Loose lips sink ships."

The cipher clerk said under his breath, 'Or cake.'

This was a simple coded check. Bert thought for a moment and said, 'I doubt they have Victoria Sandwich.'

The cipher clerk gave the final confirmation by saying, 'I prefer bread and butter.'

Anyone listening must have thought this a very odd conversation. Bert carefully slid a piece of paper along the bench seat; unseen by anyone. He had been looking at the KGB agent by the counter. He waited for a passing waiter to bump into them and cause a distraction. The clerk slipped the paper into a pocket hidden inside his jacket. After consuming drinks but no cakes, the men left separately. Presumably, the note contained important information that the USSR government awaited. Information that they were not wanting their secret service to be aware of.

Bert returned to the office, having never read the note, knowing only that he had carried out his duty. Much of his work felt that way. The secret service didn't gain its name for nothing. Compartmentalisation is the key to secrecy. They only shared with an individual the things that they needed to know. As Bert entered his office, he had a task ahead that he didn't relish. But he knew it must be done.

***

Later that day, Bert called Arthur into his office and said, 'Much as I'd like to keep you working in an office forever. Being my son-in-law that is. Keep you safe and all that...'

Arthur cut in, 'I'd hate to think there was any favouritism.'

'Perish the thought,' said Bert. 'Your scores at every test are excellent. You're ideal as a desk agent. But we also need men like you out in the field. It's going to be hard for you though. Keeping it secret from Hildy.'

'Yes sir,' said Arthur. 'She has a sharp brain, picks up the on the slightest clue.'

'Doesn't she just. When she first worked at the BBC, she came across me visiting there on SIS business. I'm pretty sure she worked that out; realised I work here. I was never sure if she had the sense not to mention it; or just forgot. You know Hildy; a bit forgetful at times.'

'Yes, absolutely,' said Arthur, nodding, perhaps thinking of the previous week. Then he asked, 'Will I have to travel abroad?'

'No, I've got a complex mission for you that's all based over here. There's a criminal gang headed by Lucian Kendall. It has fingers in hotels and businesses all over Great Britain. Kendall's a right piece of work. Clever man, keeps in with all the right people. The police can't pin anything on him, but they suspect him of blackmail, extortion, murder, you name it. Not that we have an interest in any of that of course. We leave that to them. Our interest is his potential links to the KGB. We need to know what those links are. What he's up to. If they're using him to gain access to his contacts in Britain? Or he's just using their clout? Your mission will be to investigate him and if necessary lead the team that takes him down. Are you in?'

'Rodger that sir.'

'He has a hotel down in Plympton-on-Sea called the Astoria, uses it as his base, lives there with his second wife, Debbie, and a daughter from his first marriage, Penelope. Best place to start I reckon. But you'll need to be quick on your toes. There have been rumours he's planning a move to the US.'

The one thing Bert had missed, probably because he was unaware of the full extent. Was that Lucian Kendall also had many members of the establishment in his pocket. Some through blackmail and others just thought he was innocent; part of their club. For a criminal, Lucian Kendall had friends in high places. He had an interesting past:

1895

Lucian Kendall had not always lived in such a delightful place as the luxury hotel in Plympton-on-Sea. He was born in much more lowly circumstances. Back in 1895, Lucian was born to a family of tobacconists in the East End of London. His parents had him working in their shop from a young age. Each night Lucian repeated a mantra to himself in his tatty bed, staring up at the cracked ceiling, 'I will not be shopkeeper all my life.'

1918

Whether the mantra or sheer determination worked, Lucian didn't remain a shopkeeper. He fought hard; no one stood in his way. In the First World War, he showed bravery and skill with every weapon; including his bare hands. Surviving where so many died. After punching a senior officer, Lucian Kendall could have faced a court martial, but his actions of saving the same officer's life a few days earlier led to his pardon. The officer he had saved spoke up for him. Kendall gained a medal rather than facing the firing squad.

Back on civvy street, Lucian used his fists to work his way up from minor gangs to the bigger players. The bosses recognised him as a man they could trust; perhaps their folly. He certainly had a strength and charisma that people followed. Once he became part of one of London's biggest gangs, he quickly became one of its key players. Ruthlessness gave him the edge and before long he had gained a place in the inner circle of the most notorious gang.

In 1918, at age twenty-three, Lucian made his move. No one would have guessed such a young man could become so powerful so quickly. A life on the streets had aged and hardened him. Natural confidence gave him an air of one much older. Having gathered a group of those who feared rather than trusted him, he took out the gang's leader and became head of London's most notorious criminal gang. Within a few years, he had either removed or joined with most of his competitors. The name of Lucian Kendall became one that caused many sleepless nights for those who stood against him. Anyone who tried didn't last long.

1920

In 1920, Lucian met a woman who would change his life forever. Victoria Worth was born in Connecticut, USA. But after she fell pregnant, her well connected and wealthy family had cast her aside. The father of her child, Warren Campbell, paid to send her to England. Victoria arrived in London with only the envelope of money he gave her; it didn't last long. A kindly woman took Victoria to Kilburn Maternity Home for unmarried mothers. In 1920, the only option an unmarried mother had was to give up her children for adoption. When Victoria gave birth to twins, Pearl, and Ruby, circumstances forced her to give them up for adoption. Mr and Mrs Davies adopted Ruby, they emigrated to Marlan, Ohio. Mr and Mrs Parker adopted Pearl, and they later moved next door to Hilda Shilton. The two became best friends.

It was shortly after leaving the maternity home, destitute and desperate, that Victoria met Lucian Kendall. He could see beyond the shabby clothes and dirt to a woman born to higher things. She saw a saviour rather than who he really was; a street thug. Lucian never showed his harsh or violent side to Victoria. He was smart enough to see her as his way into high society. Victoria taught Lucian proper manners; how to speak and act the part. His lowly past became hidden. When people Victoria and Lucian, they found saw a charming couple. She helped him to gain power and influence among the rich and powerful. His influence and power spread with her help. She innocently helped him spread his evil tentacles into high society.

1927

In 1927, Lucian and Victoria were secretly married in Kensal Green, London. Everyone had assumed they were already a couple; this merely formalised the arrangement. The marriage took place a short distance from Victoria's daughter Pearl and Pearl's best friend, Hilda. But none of them knew of each other. Indeed, in 1927, Hilda and Pearl had yet to meet. Life is so strange. All these people who would play such a key part in each other's lives, living so close to each other. Yet Hilda and Pearl wouldn't meet till 1928.

Hilda and Pearl didn't discover about Pearl's adoption and her twin sister, Ruby, until 1997. In that same year, they heard about Lucian Kendal. But there was one more player in this drama born in 1927 who Hilda and Pearl knew nothing of until 1997. Lucian and Victoria Kendall had a daughter, Penelope. That made her the half sister of Pearl and Ruby.

We cannot consider a baby as a criminal. Penelope was born like any other child, an innocent. But Lucian Kendall saw his only daughter Penelope as his natural successor and trained her from the youngest age in every aspect of his criminal enterprise. Young Penelope had no chance. That was also the downfall of Lucian's marriage.

1937

At ten years old, Penelope would often talk about her dad's criminal activities. Lucian was an effective teacher. He drummed his lessons in well. So that Penelope would repeat her lessons often throughout the day. At breakfast she'd say, 'Dad says heads crack as easy as these eggs.'

Her mother, Victoria, thought Penelope had misunderstood Humpty Dumpty. She said to her daughter, 'I'm sure your father said no such thing.'

One time, on a walk, Penelope noticed a woman have her bag snatched and said, 'Dad says we get a percentage of all thefts in this neighbourhood.'

Victoria had stopped; stock still and stared at her daughter. Then asked her to explain exactly what Lucian had been teaching her. At first Victoria refused to believe it, thinking it the imaginings of a child.

Later that day, she challenged Lucian and saw the truth in his eyes. That night, she tried to take Penelope to safety, but the plan failed. Penelope called to her dad for help and Victoria escaped without her daughter. She returned to the USA, once again alone. Penelope grew up with only her dad's criminal influence. The poor child had little chance of growing up as anything other than a criminal mastermind herself.

August 1948

Plympton-On-Sea, Somershire, UK

Eleven years later, Lucian Kendall married Dianne, the sister of his deputy manager, John Keighley. By this point Lucian had moved down to live in one of the hotels he now owned, the Astoria Hotel in Plympton-on-Sea. But he was getting ready to move across to the USA and hand over the management of all his UK enterprises to his brother-in-law, John Keighley.

New markets were opening in the United States and he felt England was the past for him. His twenty-one-year-old daughter Penelope was living with him and attending finishing school. She had made friends with Jayne, the future Duchess of Somershire. Lucian agreed to allow Penelope to continue her education at the finishing school in Austria. Then stay for the holidays at the Astoria. Just visiting him in the USA for longer holidays.

End of December 1948

SIS, Whitehall, London, UK

Unbeknown to SIS, by the end of December, Lucian had already left for America. He had brought forward his planned move to the USA. So when Bert sent Arthur down to the Astoria Hotel, fully expecting to find Lucian in residence. Instead, he would find Lucian had already left. But there was plenty of time for him to find that out.

Scotland Yard, London, UK

Meanwhile, across at Scotland Yard, the fog had descended again, in more ways than one. Chief Inspector Loughty looked blankly out of the window of his office. Questioning all the Italian criminals and any Italians that Loughty didn't like the look of; had been a complete waste of time – surprisingly. Humblecut's gentle persuasion had prevented Loughty from extending his enquiries to every Italian in London; Loughty reluctantly agreed that was wise. Although he reserved that as an idea for the future.

As Loughty sat in his office, he felt as dreary as the weather. Flexing his muscles wasn't helping. He had no new ideas. Not unusual for him. What he needed was fresh inspiration. He got up and headed out of his office, towards Humblecut's abode within Scotland Yard. Arriving at the office Humblecut shared with several other sergeants, Loughty filled the doorway and glanced around. There was no sign of his sergeant. He asked one of the other sergeants, 'Where's Humble?'

The sergeant Loughty had asked, glanced up at the hulk addressing him and said, 'Umm, out, I think.'

Another, more informed sergeant told Loughty that Humblecut was out pursuing leads. This annoyed Loughty. They were leads he knew nothing about. He felt peeved at his sergeant. One thing he hated was being left out of anything. So he decided on a trip to the local pub. A drink should clear his head. Why do so many detectives assume that alcohol will help them think? Doesn't it do the exact opposite?

Loughty was soon sitting in a haze of alcohol induced fug, discovering that the five pints he had consumed were not clearing his thoughts. Instead, he found the picture of hunting horses and hounds on the pub wall far more fascinating than usual. It seemed as if the horses were galloping along. Loughty could hear the red-coated riders toot their horns and see the distant fox disappear under a hedge. 'You finished?' asked the barman.

'Eh?' asked Loughty.

He stared through bleary eyes up at the expectant barman. They were pointing at his empty glass and said, 'Only it's last orders.'

'Nother pint,' said Loughty, unclearly.

'You sure?'

'Yessss, course,' said Loughty.

The barman shook his head and fetched a last pint for Loughty. Oddly, it didn't add to the clarity of thought for the chief inspector.

Chapter Seven

That Same Day

Alley by Carvey Michaels, London, UK

Thinking far more clearly than his boss, Sergeant Humblecut had been back at the scene of the crime that day. Unfortunately, he had been unable to see clearly as the fog was back. He'd missed the day without fog. Loughty had taken Humblecut off on a fool's errand around various Italian 'leads' on the clear day. But Humblecut was sure that they had missed something at the crime scene and so he stood quietly, staring into the fog. One good thing; he could see further than on the day the body had been discovered. A movement caught his eye, and he headed towards it. 'Who's there,' he asked.

'Just a poor marquess, down on his luck.'

'A marquess?'

The marquess appeared from the fog, bowed, and said, 'The Marquess of Messex at your service.'

'What are you doing here?' asked Humblecut.

'I live here dear sir.'

'Were you here on the night of the murder?' asked Humblecut.

'Ah, another bright spark I see, not like that dim witted big chap.'

'Another?' asked Humblecut.

Ignoring the jibe at his boss. The marquess nodded and said, 'Mrs Hilda Shilton of course. She was here the other day and seemed pleased with what I told her.'

'What did you tell her?' asked Humblecut.

The marquess then told Humblecut everything he had told Hilda. Well, presumably he did. That's certainly what he said he was doing to the sergeant. But memory is a funny thing and people can re tell things in different ways. Or choose to omit things. People are the most unreliable witnesses.

Kilburn, London, UK

That night at Arthur and Hilda's cosy little house, Arthur was fidgeting on the sofa. Hilda stopped dancing, looked down at him and said, 'If you're going to jiggle around you should have said yes to dancing with me earlier.'

'No, I'm happy here darling,' said Arthur.

'What is the matter with you?' asked Hilda.

'Nothing,' said Arthur. 'Although, perhaps I ought to mention that I'm away for a couple of days, on business. Have I told you that yet?'

'No, when are you going?'

'Tomorrow.'

'Tomorrow?' said Hilda. 'Oh dear, I haven't done the ironing. I'll need to check you have enough shirts.'

She pirouetted out of the room. 'Two will be fine,' shouted Arthur.

'Two,' shouted Hilda from the hallway. 'Gosh, I'm not sure I have two ready,'

Hilda danced down the corridor and up the stairs. She needed to check the washing. Hilda and the housework were not good friends. In fact, they were hardly on speaking terms most of the time. Arthur normally did the washing and ironing. Something which would have caused his late mother to spin in her grave and his work colleagues to laugh. But Arthur enjoyed such things and couldn't understand why society saw it differently. The problem was that the last few days he had been working late; very late. All to get ready for the trip down to Plympton-on-Sea. He had told Hilda his late evenings were due to an audit, but really he was doing firearms training on the first night. Then the next night he had to check he was up to date with writing and reading the latest codes and operating his field radio. One wonders how in later years, a certain secret agent, JB, got so much time to gamble, drive fast cars, spend time with beautiful women and eat in fancy restaurants. That was not the case in 1948 for poor Arthur. He had been far too busy to keep on top of his normal household chores; much less have any fun. Mind you, the fictional JB would be a bachelor. Real secret agents had real lives with families and houses to keep clean. At least Arthur did. Maybe he wasn't typical.

We'd better get back to Hilda. She was standing in their bedroom, contemplating how on earth to get enough clean clothes for her husband's trip. She had always assumed it was she who kept the wash basket empty and the cupboards full of ironed clothes. Or maybe she assumed the household fairies did it. Now as she stood in front of the wardrobe and checked on Arthur's shirts, Hilda could see that the washday fairies had been slacking. Hilda shouted down the stairs to Arthur, 'We may have a tiny problem with your shirts.'

SIS, Whitehall, London, UK

Next day at his office Arthur arrived with a tiny suitcase; he had no need for a large one. Between the two of them, Hilda and Arthur had just managed to find two clean and pressed shirts, apart from the one Arthur was wearing. Even this miracle of packing had involved a joint late night washing and ironing session. Bert stared at his son-in-laws small case and asked, 'You all set?'

'Yes sir,' said Arthur.

'You have enough clothes in there?' asked Bert. 'I know I said a couple of days. But better to be prepared.' Arthur shrugged and Bert continued, 'Ah, I see, my daughter didn't have many shirts ready. Never was much at housework. Her mother always said she'd do well to find a husband who'd take her... oh sorry old chap.'

'I love your daughter sir,' said Arthur. 'Housework is not as important as love.'

'Whatever you say old man,' said Bert. 'Here's the rest of what you'll need.'

Bert handed Arthur his 'spy' kit. A small radio, code book, and binoculars. It was lacking any exploding watches, cyanide pills, or pens that fire darts. Arthur asked, 'What about a gun sir?'

'You'll have to pop down to ordinance and sign one out,' said Bert. 'Ever since the war ended the bureaucrats are increasing the paperwork. I can't even keep one in my desk anymore. If the KGB gets past Fred on the door, I've got nothing to shoot at them with.'

Arthur stared at his father-in-law in horror. Then realised he was joking. At least he hoped he was.

Plympton-On-Sea, Somershire, UK

Being a field agent had its perks. The first being that Arthur got the use of a car. It wasn't a sports car. Arthur wondered how spies in movies got fancy cars. But at least Arthur had the use of a car and that was brill. He was making plans to use it at the weekend with Hilda. They had yet to tell him it was only for use during a job. What's often called a pool car.

Arthur motored along in his old Austin Morris. We won't say sped along; that would be exaggerating at thirty miles an hour. Considering its state, Arthur was pleased the old motor didn't break down. One thing is certain: the car didn't have any rocket launchers, ejector seats, or machine guns. Later spies might have such things, but not Arthur. Not only was it not bullet proof, Arthur doubted it was even rain proof.

***

Arthur arrived at Plympton-on-Sea. In the 1940s, it was a very different place to later years. The High Street had grocer shops, butchers, bakers, not a candlestick maker, but two dressmakers and three banks. These had all closed by the 1990s when Hilda and Pearl moved there to run a tearoom. In the 1940s, there were three tea shops. But none of them were where The Hidden Garden's Tearoom stood in 1998; that was the name of Hilda and Pearl's tearoom. Back in 1948, that location was a cottage belonging to a retired colonel and his wife. The only shop surviving from the 1940s was the post office. Although this had changed beyond all recognition. The harbour in 1948 still had a profitable fishing fleet. The few tourists who ventured into the fishermen's domain had to fight their way past piles of nets and lobster pots. Not to mention the dangers of swinging cranes. The fishermen's wives sat around low tables and sorted the catch ready for the market. All a far cry from the quaint tourist destination of later years.

Lucian Kendall's hotel, 'The Astoria Hotel, and Golf Club' was popular for two reasons. First, its golf course, outside of Scotland it boasted one of the finest in the land. Second, the promenade at Plympton, built by the Victorians, was just alongside the hotel. Hilda would certainly agree that the promenade was a fine thing. In later years she loved to dance along it. In the 1940s, the Astoria boasted incredible sea views. This was a hotel to attract the whole family. If visitors had been aware that a notorious criminal owned it, using it to launder his ill-gotten gains, they may have viewed it differently. But Lucian Kendall was careful to keep his criminal side secret. The few people who knew he owned it; saw of him as a well-connected businessman.

Friend of the local councillors, landed gentry, the Police Constable of Somershire, and several judges.

Even before Lucian moved to America, people seldom saw him in person at the hotel. He always left the day to day managing to others. When he moved, he chose a manager that was outwardly clean. John Keighley, that chosen manager, walked around his domain like a prince admiring his castle. Pompous would be an excellent description of Keighley.

***

John Keighley arrived at the hotel's front desk as Arthur Shilton was in the process of checking in. 'Here you go Mr Smith, your keys to the penthouse,' said the receptionist.

Perhaps SIS needed to train its agents in more creative aliases. Arthur Shilton, alias Mr Smith, followed the porter with his baggage to the lift. The lift operator opened the doors and took them to the top floor. After showing Mr Smith the room and receiving his tip, the porter left. Arthur glanced appreciatively around the room. He had pulled strings with SIS finance to pay for such a luxury room on one criterion. It had brilliant views of the hotel entrance, car park, golf course and, though not relevant, a decent view of the sea to the right. All this was possible from its wrap around balcony. The room was at the top of the hotel and took up a good part of that floor. Its balcony had satisfied both golfers and sea lovers. The fact it also gave magnificent views down towards the hotel grounds gave Arthur the excuse he needed. He knew of the Astoria and this incredible room from his honeymoon. Bert and Henrietta, Hilda's parents, had treated them to a long weekend here. Hilda had said, 'Well, I must say, I can get used to this.'

But Arthur and Hilda had not been able to afford such luxury again.

***

At dinner that evening, Arthur sat looking out at the golf course. The dining room in which he sat would change little over the next sixty years. Neither would the golf course. Indeed, the large lake in its centre, that caught so many golfers out, would still be there until 1999. At which point the hotel would change it. Arthur was blissfully unaware that the water he was staring at would be his grave. Not only his grave; but one he would share. For now, Mr Smith, as the waiter knew him, ordered dinner.

The manager John Keighley always liked to ensure that his important guests were well looked after. How much more important than a man staying in the penthouse? John glided over to Mr Smith's table in that way managers seem to practise and said, 'I do hope everything is satisfactory?'

The faux Mr Smith looked up and said, 'Yes, thankyou. Sorry, I don't know your name?'

John Keighley bowed and said, 'Mr John Keighley, the manager of this fine establishment, at your service.'

'The manager? But I thought...' Arthur caught himself.

No paperwork listed Lucian Kendall as part of the Astoria. But the name John Keighley appeared as a junior manager. Keighley smiled at the pretend Mr Smith and said, 'Were you expecting my predecessor, Mr Grantly perhaps?'

'Yes, that's it,' said Arthur quickly, relieved he hadn't slipped up.

'I'm so sorry,' said Keighley. 'I was unaware that you knew, Mr Grantly. Nor that you'd stayed here before. Do you know him from elsewhere?'

Arthur realised his error and said, 'You have an incredible golf course here.'

He turned towards the window and waved at the course. Keighley followed Arthur's gaze and said, 'Ah, you've not seen it before? You really must play a round. I assume you play?'

'Of course. It was kind of you to check on me,' said Arthur dismissively.

Keighley took the hint and left. He headed to one of his staff and said, 'Check on Mr Smith, the penthouse. He doesn't seem quite right.'

The staff member Keighley spoke to appeared to be a waiter. Yet he left the dining room immediately and headed upstairs. Within seconds, he was inside the penthouse room and investigating every part. Then he returned downstairs and made a few phone calls. After that, he re-entered the dining room and waved to Keighley. The two men went into Keighley's office, where the supposed waiter said, 'Mr Smith seems genuine. Except, for a rich man who can afford a penthouse room he only has two clean shirts and none of his clothes are high quality. He also has a cheap car. My contacts say he is a rich business owner. Some rich folk can be be like that. They like to act poor, or he could be someone else. Take your choice.'

'Keep an eye on him, see if he does anything suspicious,' said Keighley.

Chapter Eight

Just before Christmas 1948

Scotland Yard, London, UK

Humblecut's encounter with the Marquess of Messex had left him with a problem. He knew he should tell his boss about the meeting and what was said. But after the farrago a few days earlier of chasing after most of the Italians in London; Humblecut was reluctant. The information he had gained may send Loughty off in yet another crazy direction. The information needed checking out first. Maybe Humblecut was finally gaining some gumption. It was certainly unlike him to act on his own initiative so much.

***

Meanwhile, unaware that his junior officer was deciding on things without him, Chief Inspector Loughty made his own decision. It was nearly Christmas, and in his view, no progress was being made on the case. He would take some much needed time off. Loughty just upped and offed without a by or leave to anyone. Pretty typical of him. Humblecut turned up next morning and found a note saying that his boss would be back in the New Year. He took this as a sign he was right not to tell his boss about meeting the marquess. Then Humblecut used the peace and quiet to investigate the Father Christmas murder thoroughly. Christmas came and went with Humblecut, able to spend the time happily investigating alone.

Beginning January 1949

Kilburn, London, UK

January can be such a dire month. Christmas has passed and the bills are in. Often, the weather is dreary. But Hilda skipped along Kilburn High Road looking as if she hadn't a care in the world. She was singing, 'Oh what a beautiful morning.'

This was not very appropriate, as clouds hung heavily in the sky, and rain threatened. As Hilda danced along, something dampened her spirits. Not the rain; that had yet to start. It was the sight of so many gaps in the road where houses used to stand. It reminded her of bombing during the war, which had destroyed vast swathes of London.

After the war, the government had started a speedy re-building project, but the scale of the problem in places like London was immense. There were still bomb sites surrounded by makeshift fencing everywhere you went. Kids saw these areas as dangerous adventure playgrounds and braved the unexploded bomb warnings. As the brave or foolish youngsters explored the ruins, they had the bonus of finding many hidden treasures among the rubble. Children didn't appreciate the horror, nor the fact these were once other people's precious treasures. To them, it was all one giant playground.

As Hilda danced past one large hole in a fence, a young lad ran out, treasure in hand. He bumped into Hilda and shouted, 'Sorry missus.'

Hilda stopped and watched the young lad run onwards, clutching an armful of books. She looked down at her feet. The collision had caused the lad to drop a couple of the books. Hilda bent down and picked them up. They weren't obvious reading for such a young lad. Perhaps he'd stumbled across a bombed library and hoped to sell the books he found. The first book was a rather fine leather-bound book. Hilda opened it and read the inscription within:

The diary of Victoria Kendall, Nee Worth.

Hilda realised this was not a discovery from a bombed out library. But the personal diary of some poor soul, perhaps killed in the bombing of her home. Hilda sighed and placed the diary in her bag. This was many years before Hilda would discover that Victoria Worth was her best friend, Pearl's natural mother. Oh well, perhaps something may jog her memory in many years' time. How many times must we come across significant things that mean nothing to us at the time? Perhaps they never become relevant to us; but have great meaning if only we knew why. Life is a tapestry of overlapping coincidences.

Hilda glanced at the other book. It had a black cover with no writing on it. When Hilda opened it, she could see it was a ledger of some sort. Flicking through it, she saw dates, numbers, and initials. Numbers always turned her cold; ever since school. That book quickly joined the other in her bag. Once she reached home, she placed them both on a bookshelf and promptly forgot about them.

Plympton-On-Sea, Somershire, UK

That same morning, at the Astoria Hotel, Hilda's husband, Arthur, was working hard; at least he was doing his job. Which involved sitting on the balcony of his room and observing the activities at the hotel. Some might see that as a simple job, especially as he'd convinced himself that to look innocent; he needed to be drinking and eating. It was a bitter January day, so he was drinking a hot toddy and eating a slice of toast. The toast remained from breakfast – it was only 10 am. Quite how he justified drinking alcohol so early, one cannot say. But then, certain famous secret agents never had a problem with that in later years. So perhaps Arthur was a trendsetter. The names Arthur, Arthur Shilton, I'll have a hot toddy, shaken, not stirred; maybe not.

The golf course was quiet; not surprising on such a wintry day. Sea fog was just rolling in. A golfer would find it hard to see a ball, much less direct it towards a hole. Arthur shivered and took another sip of his hot toddy. Then noticed a vehicle pull up in the car park. He nodded to himself and felt justified in his decision to sit on the balcony, eating and drinking. Arthur watched four men get out of the car. One advantage of fog is the way it reflects sound. One of the men spoke in Russian. The other angrily told him to speak English. They looked around; but not upwards. Thinking they had escaped notice, they continued into the hotel. Arthur headed downstairs, hoping to get a closer look at the new arrivals.

The four men from the car park were sitting at a table in the dining area. John Keighley had just joined them as Arthur walked into the dining room. Arthur kept to the far side of the room and found a table. He sat with his back to them. The room was nearly empty as the hotel wasn't busy and most guests had already enjoyed breakfast. A waiter took Arthur's order for a pot of tea. While waiting for his drink, Arthur sat and listened. The men spoke too quietly for him to overhear more than the occasional sentence; all spoken in English. But Arthur had heard enough outside to be certain these men were Russian and, in his view, that made them likely agents. The bits he overheard were not the conversations of businessmen or holidaymakers.

SIS, Whitehall, London, UK

Next day, Bert Shilton stood in front of his boss, Commander Jameson. Bert had just handed Jameson a telegram from his son-in-law, Arthur. After reading it, Jameson looked up and said, 'How certain is he they're KGB?'

'He has little to go on, a snatch of Russian language and a brief mention of an operation they're planning. But he couldn't hear the details.'

Jameson nodded and said, 'We can't act on so little. Tell him to gather more evidence.'

'Will do,' said Bert.

'By the way,' said Jameson. 'The message you passed on has been received and acted upon.'

'I don't suppose...' started Bert.

'No, it's contents are way above your level,' said Jameson. 'But know you've played a key role.'

'Thank you sir,' said Bert.

As he left on route to contact Arthur, he again wondered about the high level machinations of government. On one hand, they were trying to bring down a suspected KGB cell in the South of England. On the other, they were communicating with the enemy like friends.

Scotland Yard, London, UK

The next day, an invigorated Chief Inspector Loughty breezed into his sergeant's office and asked, 'Right, Humble, where are we on this daft case with the man who likes dressing up in Father Christmas suits?'

Humblecut looked up and said, 'I have some interesting information regarding that sir.'

'Do you indeed? Let's hear it.'

'Just before Christmas I returned to the scene of the murder...'

'Who told you to do that?' Cut in Loughty.

The tone caused Humblecut to draw a sharp breath. A couple of the other sergeants who shared the office with Humblecut were listening in. They shook their heads; perhaps glad Loughty wasn't their boss. Humblecut stood slowly and said to his boss, 'If you could perhaps wait a moment sir, I'll tell you the outcome.'

Loughty growled and said, 'Right, carry on.'

He walked closer to Humblecut; towering above him. Humblecut glanced up at his boss, then said, 'Thank you sir. When I was there I met The Marquess of Messex.'

'I thought you were visiting the same back alley as before, not hobnobbing in London clubs. I'd have come along if you had planned that.'

Loughty's voice was even sharper. The other sergeants looked away; studiously carrying on with their work. Humblecut said, 'No sir, it was nothing like that. The marquess has had a run of bad luck. He's now living in that alley.'

'A marquess living in an alleyway? That's not cricket,' said Loughty.

He looked like he'd been slapped round the face. His entire world view had turned upside down. The revelation seemed to take the edge from his voice. Loughty sank into a chair. Humblecut hesitated for a moment and then said, 'Shocking I know. But it's a fact.'

Loughty glanced up, distracted, and then said, 'What is the world coming to? We beat Hitler and now the best in the land are out in the gutter.'

The two other sergeants in the room got up and left. When Loughty shook his head sadly. Humblecut nodded and said, 'The marquess said something similar himself sir. But, he did notice something helpful on the night of the murder.'

Loughty wasn't listening to his sergeant and said, 'I know who I'd sling out on their ears into some back alley.'

'I'm not sure if you heard me sir?' asked Humblecut.

'What's that?' asked Loughty.

'The marquess heard something on the night of the murder,' said Humblecut.

Loughty turned to his sergeant, sighed and said, 'A man of quality is bound to be a help; even when he's on his uppers. I must meet this gentleman.'

'Do you want to hear what he said first?' asked Humblecut.

'I'll hear it from the man himself,' said Loughty. 'It's important that such a man has a chance to know he can still be being helpful to his majesty's constabulary.'

As they walked out, Humblecut muttered something about the marquess already being aware of that fact.

Alley by Carvey Michaels, London, UK

Chief Inspector Loughty and Sergeant Humblecut arrived on a clear day at the alleyway. The sun glittered in the muddy puddles. Old crates threw shadows across the alley in pleasing patterns. A broken glass bottle twinkled beautifully... anyway you get the picture. The day differed greatly from their last visit. As the two officers strode up the alley, a cat ran across their path, causing Humblecut to jump. Well, he was a bit on edge after the discussion at the office. Loughty stared at his sergeant in disgust and asked, 'Where is this refined gentleman? Why ever are we in this muddy alley again?'

'He was over here,' said Humblecut. He walked towards a recessed area part way down the alley. Loughty followed his sergeant, and they both stood staring at a pile of clothing and blankets. 'Sorry sir, he's not here,' said Humblecut unnecessarily.

'I should think not,' said Loughty.

'Fancy seeing you here,' said Hilda, from behind them.

She was walking into the alleyway with her new friend, the Marquess of Messex. Hilda had taken him for a cup of tea and a slice of toast at a local cafe. The chief inspector glanced up at Hilda and her scruffy friend. He sniffed, not just in dismissal, but in disgust at the smell emanating from the marquess. 'I'm terribly sorry, my dear man,' said the marquess. 'I'm not my usual self. The facilities around here are rather lacking. But my kind friend Mrs Shilton has been treating me at a local hostelry.'

Loughty stared at the marquess and said, 'I don't care what you've been up to, you scruffy oik. Humble, get these two out of here and find The Marquess of Messex.'

'Umm, well you see sir,' said Humblecut.

The Marquess of Messex walked up to Loughty; dirty hand outstretched and said, 'A pleasure to meet you my good man.'

The chief inspector looked outraged and stepped backwards, tripping over a box and falling into the mud. The marquess said, 'My word, you'll be as messy as me before long.'

Hilda giggled. Humblecut struggled not to smile and helped his boss up. Loughty shouted, 'Get rid of them now Humble.'

'But sir, this is the Marquess of Messex,' said Humblecut.

Loughty rose, dripping water and mud, mouth wide open. The marquess grabbed his hand and shook it. Then the marquess realised that he had picked up more mud from the chief inspector than was already on his own hands. The marquess wiped his mucky hands on his trouser leg. An exercise in futility. Then he asked Loughty, 'Who do I have the pleasure of meeting?'

'I'm, umm, well, err...' started Loughty.

Hilda helped and said, 'This is the world famous glove detective. If you ever lose any clothing you can call on him. I am assured he is an expert in haberdashery.'

'Now that's not fair Mrs Shilton,' said Humblecut, hiding a smile.

***

A short while later, Hilda, the Marquess of Messex and the two detectives were sitting in a nearby cafe. It was a different one to the place Hilda had taken the marquess. This second cafe owner had been unhappy to allow two 'tramps' as he called them, access. He lumped Loughty together with the marquess, due to his dishevelled state. But after the police officers showed him their warrant cards, the cafe owner recanted and allowed them a table - at the back.

'This is most kind of you,' said the marquess. 'Two cups of tea in one morning, unheard of. Next you'll be buying me cake.'

He eyed a cake at the counter. But Loughty was preoccupied and failed to notice the hint. Humblecut was about to say something, but Loughty jumped in first and said, 'I am so sorry for the confusion earlier, your lordship, Mrs Shilton has interfered in our investigation before.'

Hilda said, 'I beg your pardon?'

The marquess said, 'Really? I find Mrs Shilton to be a most intelligent and helpful young woman. Perhaps you should be seeking her help; rather than dismissing it?'

Hilda smiled at the marquess. Loughty ground his teeth. Then, turning to the marquess, Loughty said, 'If you wish. But we don't generally call upon amateurs, your lordship.'

'You really don't need to be so formal,' said the marquess. 'I am rather on my uppers at the moment.'

'A terrible fact and one I would change if I had the power,' said Loughty.

He wafted his hand in a manner that suggested a magic trick, royal decree, or perhaps benediction. The marquess smiled and said, 'Thank you chief inspector.'

Humblecut said, 'Could you please tell the chief inspector what you told me about the night of the murder.'

'Listen carefully,' said Hilda. 'You will then know almost as much as me.'

Loughty stared at Hilda in disgust.

Chapter Nine

Beginning January 1949

A small cafe in London, UK

The Marquess of Messex took a sip of his tea, glanced again at the cakes, and then said, 'Now, let me see, ah yes, that bleak and foggy night just before Christmas, It really drove the cold into my bones.'

'I know what you mean,' said Hilda. 'I said to Pearl, it was such a good idea we bought that thermal underwear.'

Loughty and Humblecut stared at Hilda in horror. Then the marquess continued, 'Yes, well, I suppose so dear lady.'

Hilda asked him, 'Gambling wasn't it?'

'What's that?' asked Loughty.

Hilda looked at Loughty and said, 'It was gambling that caused the marquess to lose everything. Why he just has the clothes he stands up in.'

'Ah, now, you see,' said the marquess. 'I did have a slight problem...'

'You don't have to answer that your lordship,' said Loughty, cutting in.

'That's what you told me,' said Hilda. 'Didn't he tell you that Rumplestiltskin?'

'My names Humblecut, and it's not exactly what he said to me,' Humblecut turned to the marquess and said, 'You mentioned investment problems.'

Hilda shook her head and said, 'Investments, really? That's not how you explained it to me. Anyway, you lost all your money, by one means or another.'

'You don't have to listen to this your lordship,' said Loughty.

'It's alright,' said the marquess, hanging his head. 'Mrs Shilton is right. I made mistakes, gambled too heavily, with the wrong people. So yes, dear lady, I only have what you see now. But I was sensible. I remembered my army training. Lots of layers and a thick balaclava. Then my waterproof gabardine coat on top.'

'Very sensible your lordship, I'm army man myself,' said Loughty. 'You never forget do you?'

They swapped a few regimental tales. After they had finished their stories, Hilda said, 'Didn't you say that you joined a few other homeless men under an old railway arch? Ones with a fire in a metal drum.'

'You didn't tell me that,' said Humblecut.

'That because I generally avoided them,' said the marquess. 'My accent and background seemed to cause problems. Besides, I enjoyed being on my own.'

'What about the night of the murder?' asked Loughty. 'That's if it's alright with you to talk about it your lordship? I wouldn't want to cause you any embarrassment.'

'It's a murder,' said Hilda. 'You can't go worrying about hurting his feelings.'

'You are only here because I am allowing it,' said Loughty. 'So just keep quiet.'

'How very rude you are,' said Hilda.

'It's alright my good man,' said the marquess. 'There's no need to harangue the dear lady. I am happy to talk.'

'There you go,' said Hilda.

Loughty opened his mouth to speak, but must have thought better of it. The marquess said, 'I was trying to sleep and failing; it's very difficult you know when it's so very cold.'

'I think it's disgraceful,' said Loughty. 'A man of your background.'

'Yes quite,' said the marquess. 'The nights I've lain awake shivering in the cold. Even with all these layers. Not enough blankets you know? I wish I had a fire.'

Humblecut nodded in agreement. Perhaps he had more recent memories of a cold office in mind. Hilda asked, 'Didn't you see something or someone?'

'You're right young lady. I was woken by a sound. Not that I was really sleeping and I saw a shadowy figure of a man in red enter the alleyway.'

'Father Christmas?' asked Loughty.

'He certainly resembled that seasonal chappie,' said the marquess.

'Aha,' said Loughty. 'Now we're getting somewhere. What else did you see?'

'A red glow,' said the Marquess.

'A red glow?' asked Loughty. 'What, in the sky?'

'No, no, dear chap. Around his face. It lit up his rosy cheeks and bushy white beard. It told me he was smoking,' said the marquess.

'Definitely the Father Christmas look alike,' said Hilda.

'Yes, of course, we all know that.' said Loughty. 'Anything else your lordship?'

'He disappeared,' said the marquess. 'At least, I don't know if it was the fog increasing or me falling asleep. But the man disappeared.'

'What vanished?' asked Loughty.

'Well, I didn't see him for a while. But maybe ten minutes later. I no longer have a pocket watch you understand? There was shouting,' said the marquess.

'What was said?' asked Loughty.

'I don't listen in on people,' said the marquess.

'Of course not your lordship,' said Loughty. 'Not something I would expect of such a man as yourself.'

'Nevertheless, you heard something, didn't you?' said Hilda.

'Yes, I couldn't help but hear a little,' said the marquess. 'Although I wouldn't know what they were saying. Perhaps it was a foreign language. I never excelled at languages at school.'

'Me neither,' said Hilda. 'Very tricky thing; other languages. French is a complete mystery to me.'

'Very true,' said the marquess, 'I wondered if I heard the word, "dingy." Though why they'd talk about boats, I don't know. Someone may have cried out, but that could have been the cat from the alley.'

'What about when the police arrived?' asked Humblecut.

Everyone stared at him in surprise. The marquess then said, 'I heard Mrs Shilton arrive, then the first lot of officers and then you Mr Humblecut and your chief.'

He nodded at Loughty. The chief nodded sagely, as if everything was now clear. But his face looked blank.

'Odd you didn't make yourself know when the police arrived,' said Hilda.

'I was confused and cold,' said the marquess.

'Of course your lordship,' said Loughty. 'I'm just sorry we disturbed you with our investigations that night.'

Hilda and Humblecut stared at the chief inspector in surprise.

Plympton-On-Sea, Somershire, UK

While his wife was sitting in a cafe in London, hearing about the murder of Father Christmasses helper. Arthur was sitting in his room at the Astoria Hotel, reading a coded message from his wife's father, Bert. Or, as she called him, pops. Arthur decoded it and shook his head. How was he supposed to get evidence to prove that the KGB was definitely at the Astoria? At least without getting caught and or killed. He sat back and thought about a strategy. Planning was his forte. He just wasn't used to putting his own plans into action.

***

That night at dinner, Arthur called John Keighly over to his table and asked, 'Do you run any games?'

'Games?' asked Keighley. 'You mean golf?'

'No, card games,' said Arthur, winking.

'Ah, you mean bridge,' said Keighley, smiling like a cat.

'I meant something more interesting,' said Arthur.

He took out his wallet and flipped through a few notes. Arthur had gained special permission to withdraw extra funds for this purpose. Keighley stared at the notes with avarice and said, 'Poker?'

Arthur nodded and said, 'I assume you may know of a game somewhere around here?'

'You'll need to travel to a London casino,' said Keighley. 'We aren't licenced.'

'I wasn't looking for a licenced game,' said Arthur. 'Surely you know of a place?'

Keighley rubbed his hands, still staring at the cash. 'You don't mind it being... unlicenced?' Arthur shook his head. Keighley smiled and said, 'Perhaps I might know of one, let me make a call.' He headed off to his office and returned a short while later. 'There's a game tonight. The buy in is quite high though.'

'Sounds good to me,' said Arthur.

***

After Arthur had left, Keighley called the waiter over. The one who he had tasked with checking on Mr Smith. Keighley asked, 'What else did you find out about Mr Smith?'

'My initial suspicions were wrong. He's clean. I checked him as thoroughly as possible. Our Mr Smith is who he seems to be. A rather odd rich man, aren't they all. He hates spending money, except on gambling and fancy hotels.'

'It takes all sorts. He sounds ideal. We can use more like him. I've just sent him to a game with Pavlov,' said Keighley.

'Was Pavlov OK with that?'

'He said, so long as the guy has a lot of money to lose. Besides we get a cut of his games.' Keighley laughed. 'Seems like Pavlov's enjoying being over here a bit too much.'

'What are they really up to?' asked the faux waiter.

'Who knows; or cares,' said Keighley. 'So long as we get paid. Did you get them the weapons and explosives they wanted?'

'Sure, but it's enough to start a small war,' said the waiter.

'So long as we aren't casualties,' said Keighley.

***

In a back room at the Astoria, six men sat around a table. The air was thick with smoke and the only light came from a harsh, low light above the table. A few of the men had young women hanging around them, fetching them drinks or just sitting nearby. The others appeared more focussed on the game. Arthur walked in and swallowed hard; this was going to test all his skills. He was not brilliant at poker; but he was lucky. He approached the table and was about to explain who he was when Pavlov said, 'Mr Smith? Take a seat.'

Arthur, AKA Mr Smith, sat at a hastily vacated seat and placed his buy in money on the table. The dealer handed him chips in return. Arthur refused an offered drink and settled down to lose the first few hands. That wasn't the plan; just the way it happened. Pavlov may have assumed Mr Smith was a ringer. Playing them for fools. He certainly scrutinised the newcomer. After Arthur had lost the second hand, Pavlov said, 'Good thing you can afford to lose so much money.'

'The advantage of a successful business,' said Arthur. Pavlov snorted. Arthur asked him, 'What line are you in?'

'We play not talk,' said Pavlov.

'Absolutely, old man,' said Arthur. 'I wouldn't want to throw you off your game.'

'Your the one losin,' said Pavlov sharply.

'Very good of you to prevent me losing more,' said Arthur. 'My wife would not be pleased.'

Pavlov hesitated for a moment and then said, 'Manufacture.'

'That must be a fascinating area to work in; what do you make?'

'I'm thinking you ask many questions. Let's play,' said Pavlov.

After another two hands, Arthur had heard enough and lost enough. He needed an excuse to leave. 'Is that the time?' he said, glancing at the clock. 'I must call my wife.'

'You don't want to win back money?' asked Pavlov.

'It's only money,' said Arthur. 'Plenty more where that came from.'

He hoped Bert would be able to square things with finance. The information must be worth the outlay.

***

Back in his room, Arthur coded a message to SIS headquarters. Pavlov was definitely Russian. He spoke English well. But there were many slip-ups in his grammar; typical of Eastern Europeans. The accents were also there; but subtle. Arthur hoped this would be evidence enough. But he felt the SIS chief would want more solid proof they worked for the KGB. How could he prove that? Perhaps a quick check of their rooms while they were still playing cards; risky but worth it. Take his opportunity.

Arthur headed to the reception desk. It was empty - a fortunate occurrence. He slipped behind the desk and looked for the room numbers that matched the car registration. The names of the men listed were typical English ones. Then Arthur headed to those rooms. Picking locks was a skill he learnt at SIS. Two men occupied each of the three rooms. Arthur spent five minutes in each room; he didn't want to risk longer. He hit the jackpot in the second room. One of the men had been careless when replacing their equipment. A radio transmitter and codebook, hidden; or rather, not quite hidden in a secret panel on the wall. This hotel was built with the KGB in mind. No doubt an agreement with Lucian Kendall. Whilst the radio wasn't labelled KGB; it was obviously Eastern Bloc in manufacture. Hiding a transmitter and codebook was the proof Arthur needed. He took photos of the codebook and transmitter. Before he left the room, he found one more thing of interest; their stash of weapons. Not the arsenal they would gain soon; but a considerable number of guns. Had Arthur hung around a few more days, he would have seen the men meet a large truck full of weapons and explosives. SIS code breakers would find clues to that fact when they investigated the code book Arthur photographed. The next morning, Arthur checked out of the hotel and headed back to London.

Hilda's home, Kilburn, London, UK

After a busy day at work reporting the details of his trip to The Astoria, Arthur headed home. It would be a few days before the code breaking section reported back on the weapons arsenal. On arriving home, Arthur found Hilda had prepared a treat for their evening meal. A kind of Shepard's Pie made out of very little meat and no butter. Arthur and Hilda were well ready for rationing to end. But the enjoyment came from sharing time together.

After dinner, Hilda told Arthur he could put his feet up and she would wash up; a rare treat. He decided to read and stood at their small bookcase, selecting a title. There were a couple of new books Arthur didn't recognise. One had the inscription:

'The Diary of Victoria Kendall nee Worth.'

The name Kendall leapt out at Arthur; but he assumed it was a coincidence. The other book was just black leather. Curious, Arthur picked up the diary first. If it was Hilda's personal diary written in an old book, he would replace it immediately. But the contents shocked him. This was Lucian Kendall's wife's diary.

Arthur sat down and read it more fully. He also flicked through a few pages of the ledger. When Hilda came through fifteen minutes later, Arthur looked up and asked, 'My dearest, where did you get these books?'

Hilda walked over and glanced at the books and said, 'Some child dropped them.'

'Where? How?' asked Arthur.

Hilda explained, bumping into the child. Arthur said they were key to an investigation that her father, pops she corrected him. Pops, he then said, was carrying out. Hilda told him it was fine to take them. She promptly forgot all about them.

Chapter Ten

January 1949

Eastcote, London, UK

During WWII, there are many unsung heroes who worked at Bletchley Park in Buckinghamshire. An old country house converted into a top secret base. Books and films have highlighted many individuals for their work in code cracking the German communications during the war. But there were also many whose jobs were more mundane; less obvious. They ground away at the day-to-day code breaking. After the war, they transferred many of these code breakers, both men, and women, to Eastcote on the outskirts of London. It was here that the two books arrived, ready for interpretation and code-breaking. They had also just received the photographs Arthur took at The Astoria.

The section supervisor, Margaret, stared at the pile of papers on her desk and sighed. Mondays were not her favourite day. She picked up the first one and started an orderly pile, allocating the jobs for each girl she oversaw. Then she placed the piles in alternating directions on her tray and stood up. Walking down the row of desks, she greeted her staff and gave each their assignment. The last package contained Victoria Worth's diary and the ledger. She noticed that some photos from The Astoria Hotel appeared linked to these books. Margaret said, 'Here you are, Joan, looks an interesting mix for you to get your teeth into.'

Joan flicked through the two books and photos, then said, 'I like the numbers, but could take or leave the other bits.'

Margaret knew Joan loved any puzzle. She smiled and said, 'Look for links, hidden clues. Sounds like SIS have a bee in their bonnet on this one and the big wigs want it fast.'

'Don't they always?' asked Joan.

'I've given it to my best,' said Margaret.

She knew Joan would work fast, anyway; but encouragement never harmed. Joan shook her head and glanced at the diary first. She read the title and said, 'Odd to put her maiden name.'

'See, I told you, you're the best.'

'Trying to butter me up eh?' said Joan.

Margaret grinned and headed back to her desk. While Joan laid everything out on her desk and set to work. She could see there were links between the three pieces of information. After an initial check of the three lots of documents, she started with the diary. It would take her a while to read it all and seemed to link the other two. She read:

"The Diary of Victoria Kendall, Nee Worth"

4th August 1927

Today I married Lucian Kendall. I should be the happiest woman alive, and yet I feel uncertain. This diary is to be my place to chronicle all my thoughts and feelings. There are things happening that don't feel right and I want to record them. It's a gut feeling.

Further on Joan read:

If you are reading this, then presumably I am no longer around. You may well ask why I married Lucian. Gratitiude, thanks, security, fear. Not a fear of him, but a fear of being alone again. My family cast me out when I was only seventeen years old. A vile man, I won't speak his name, took advantage of my innocence. When my parents discovered I was pregnant, they disowned me. The man; who was married, as I then discovered, sent me to England with a small amount of money.

Then a few pages on:

I will never regret having my wonderful daughters. My regret is that I could not keep them. Hope and Faith, I named them. But I am sure their adopted parents gave them new names. They are always Hope and Faith to me. I left my lovely twin girls without my care and, once again, I was cast out. But Lucian rescued me. He asked nothing of me. Such a caring and kind man. Yes, I could see that he had a rough past. There are glimpses of his harsher side. But he is always a gentleman to me.

Joan carried on reading until she came to:

17th September 1927

Today Lucian found out some information for me. He knew that I'd want to find out about my twin daughters. Apparently, he knows someone who works at the Kilburn maternity home for unmarried mothers. Hope and Faith were both adopted and re-named. Mr and Mrs Parker adopted Hope, they renamed her Pearl. Mr and Mrs Davies adopted Faith, they renamed her Ruby. The person Lucian asked doesn't know anymore. But at least I know they have parents and that they are now called Pearl and Ruby; such treasures.

Joan made notes about the twin girls' new names. SIS might have a way to find out more. Joan also compared the diary and ledger for comparative sections. She realised the ledger had a coded date sequence. It began slightly later than the diary. She noted the code names and dates. Since she lacked access to all the names involved in the case, the SIS was investigating, she could only provide a list of initials and the dates they corresponded to.

- **GMM**

- **MLV**

- **AJK**

There were also about ten initials all beginning FC. Joan then carried on reading Victoria's diary.

There were many entries about lavish banquets. It seemed that the great and the good from England at the time saw the Kendalls as suitable friends. Or at least acquaintances. Joan noticed that a couple of the entries parralleled dates and payments in the ledger. Presumably someone at those parties was being paid off:

6th June 1936

Lord and Lady Vernon make a fuss of visiting. They brought several staff and filled all our guest and spare staff bedrooms. We held a ball in their honour tonight. Lady Vernon expressed her thanks. But I still find British people very reserved in their thanks. Lady Vernon has progressive views on women's rights. Her husband is a fossil. I saw little of him, as he spent a lot of time with Lucian.

In two weeks' time, we are going up to visit them at Wold Castle. I've always wanted to see an actual castle. When I said that to Lady Vernon, she laughed and told me it's only called Wold Castle. It's not really one.

Further on Joan read:

19th October 1936

I have an awful headache. Tonight we had a dinner party and there were more of England's landed gentry there than I ever want to see again. As if that wasn't bad enough, Lucian invited the commissioner of Scotland Yard and a few judges. It was such a squash fitting everyone in. I think Lucian enjoys showing off. He took people on tours of all his new artwork. I kept telling him that's not the done thing. But he doesn't understand. It must be his humble upbringing. I wish he'd tell me more about his past. I've never even met his parents or any of his family. They weren't at the wedding.

Then Joan came to a part about Penelope, Victoria's daughter.

10th May, 1938

Morning

This morning Penny said the most atrocious things. I still can't believe it. She made it sound as if Lucian was training her in some kind of violent endeavour. Almost as if he would want her to be a criminal. My plan is to talk to him tonight.

Evening

This is a quick note. Everything has gone wrong. I can't believe my own ears. Lucian is a criminal. He told me himself. I must escape and take Penny with me. If all goes well, I'll go back to America. I have some money saved. This diary and a ledger I found in Lucian's study will act as a record of everything. I'll hide it for now and fetch it later.

The diary ended at that point. Joan realised Victoria must have been unable to fetch the diary. She continued with decoding the ledger; then finally turned to the photographs. They held the same cipher as in the ledger and were easy to decode. Joan decoded a message about a request for guns and explosives. Then went over and handed her completed work to Margaret. 'That was fast,' said Margaret.

'You wanted it quickly,' said Joan. 'Besides, those photographs contain a coded date that is imminent.'

'Shame we don't get a bonus for speed,' said Margaret.

She rang for a messenger.

SIS, Whitehall, London, UK

The messenger delivered the decoded books with attached notes along with the decoded photographs back to SIS. Bert called

Arthur through and showed him the decoded photos first. Arthur said, 'They had a lot of guns in their room.'

Bert nodded and said, 'Sounds like they're planning a lot more. You were right about them.'

Arthur then read the decoded list in the ledger and saw all the initials FC. He immediately thought of Father Christmas, but of course, threw that idea out. Each of the payments to the initials which Joan had listed was small. So they were enough for low-level informants only. Bert and Arthur studied the ledger for a while.

Then Arthur picked up Victoria Kendall's diary. Victoria was the natural mother of Pearl Parker, a person Arthur knew well. Pearl had a twin sister named Ruby. They both had a half sister Penelope by Lucian Kendall. Arthur felt it was better not to tell Hilda or Pearl about any of this. Besides, these papers were now classified as top secret.

Arthur read the part where Victoria wrote of her early life with Lucian. How she had not realised what kind of man he was. It saddened him to read that Victoria found out who Lucian truly was when Penelope was ten years old. She had written more about his criminal empire and hidden the diary along with a stolen ledger of his day-to-day activities under her bedroom floor. Research that SIS later carried out showed Victoria escaped, alone and obviously without these books. She had returned to her home country of America; where she still lived.

Bert contacted the FBI in America, but they were unable to find Victoria. She had disappeared. In 1948, it was easier to do that. She had merely changed her name and re-married. Years later, in 1998, Pearl and Ruby would find her. At that time, she was living in a nursing home.

Bert passed everything upwards to Commander Jameson. The commander felt there was enough evidence for the police to take action about the weapons and explosives. But he wanted to keep that separate from Lucian's organisation and the KGB.

The SIS sent Arthur back to the Astoria to gather more evidence on KGB links in the UK. Arthur also needed to gather more details on the arms cache. That was their way forward. SIS was a spy organisation, not a criminal investigation unit. Whatever criminal activities Lucian had been involved in did not interest SIS. Because of the secrecy surrounding the discovered books, they chose not to inform Scotland Yard of anything. Lucian Kendall's UK criminal operation continued unhindered even while Arthur was investigating their links with the KGB. Bert told Arthur to be careful. They now knew these KGB agents were heavily armed.

Mid February 1949

Plympton-On-Sea, Somershire, UK

At the Astoria Hotel, Penelope Kendall was on a half-term break from her finishing school. She had her friend with her, Jayne Bulsam, the future Duchess of Somershire. The two young ladies acted younger than their twenty years; running and playing around the hotel. One Monday morning, they ran headlong into Arthur Shilton as he walked across the entrance lobby. 'I'm most terribly sorry young ladies,' he said.

It's an Englishman's way; apologising for things that are not their fault. The girls giggled loudly and ran on. Arthur lifted his hat and watched them leave. Then continued to the reception desk. John Keighley was manning the desk. 'Ah, Mr Smith, how nice to see you back again.'

Arthur was pleased to be reminded of his alias. Perhaps spying wasn't his thing after all. 'Yes indeed, I have more business in these parts.'

'Will you be wanting to play any more "games" while you're with us?' asked Keighley, winking.

'You know, I think I might,' said the faux Mr Smith.

'There's a game on tonight,' said Keighley.

'The same gentlemen are back here?' asked Arthur.

He tried to appear casual. But felt a mixture of excitement and panic.

'They come and go, much like yourself.'

'Tell them I'll be there.'

***

Later that night, Arthur returned to his room, having lost more treasury money. But gained SIS information and stayed alive. Pavlov had let slip that he and his colleagues, as he called them, were expecting something that night. While Pavlov said it casually, the response from one of his men demonstrated it should not have been said. Arthur decided that his best vantage point to view the arrival would be the bushes in the car park. That way, he could also hear the conversation. Arthur had received a small 16mm cine camera since his last trip. Small by 1940s standards.

Once in the car park, Arthur found a suitable place within the bushes and setup. He had a long and cold wait. Fortunately, the fog kept away that night. Arthur was sure he had not nodded off, yet he felt himself jerk into wakefulness when a van door closed. The van was nondescript, grey and had no obvious markings. As Arthur looked through the eyepiece of the cine camera and zoomed in, he tried to capture all he could. But the darkness made that tricky. The van driver had come around and was speaking to Pavlov. 'Here you go.'

'I need to check,' said Pavlov.

'It's all there,' said the driver. 'Don't you trust me?'

'I don't know you,' said Pavlov.

The driver opened the rear door. Fortunately, Arthur had positioned himself in such a way that he could film into the rear of the van. Wooden crates filled the van. One of his men leapt into the back; crowbar in hand. They levered open a box and held up a gun. 'Nice,' said the man.

'Open some more,' said Pavlov.

The man opened a few random crates and held up guns and explosives. The van driver then asked, 'Happy?'

'Yes, you can go,' said Pavlov.

The driver left. After he'd gone, one of Pavlov's men said, 'What was that?'

'A fox?' said Pavlov.

'I heard a noise,' said the man.

Arthur stopped breathing. Pavlov said, 'In a car park in the back of beyond? Your paranoid.'

'Better paranoid than dead,' said the man.

'These English idiots don't even know we're here,' said the Pavlov. 'They will sleepwalk into oblivion. While mother Russia destroys them. Just look at that idiot Arthur we fleeced earlier.'

One of the men drove the van off. Arthur ran to his car and followed. The other men walked into the hotel. Arthur followed the van all the way to a nearby warehouse. Then he headed to his car. He had the film evidence and the location of their weapons. The KGB was in the UK, not just the UK, but here in a quiet backwater. Armed and ready to cause mayhem. They were working with a criminal gang in Somershire at the Astoria Hotel. But Arthur would foil their plans.

Chapter Eleven

Mid February 1949

Hilda's home, Kilburn, London, UK

While Arthur was still in Plympton-on-Sea messing up the KGB's plans, Hilda was home and at a loose end. It was a Saturday morning, and usually Hilda and Arthur would enjoy some time together. Not wanting to miss out on a fun morning, Hilda invited Pearl over. The two ladies had already moved all the information on the Father Christmas murder from Pearl's house to Arthur and Hilda's spare room. They had found a large sheet of wood and stuck all the clipping to it. Now they stood in front of the clue board, as Hilda called it. Pearl tapped her toes, then said, 'Shall I put the kettle on?'

'You'll never make a good detective if you don't concentrate,' said Hilda.

'I don't want to be a detective, good or otherwise,' said Pearl.

'That's your problem,' said Hilda. 'You just don't focus on things.'

Pearl peered over imaginary glasses at Hilda, then said, 'I lack focus?'

'I'm glad you agree. As my pops always says, "Hildy concentrate your thoughts on your hands. After all the suns rays don't burn unless they're out of focus." I think he was quoting that telephone Chappie Mr Bell.'

Pearl shook her head and said, 'Hilda, you really need to...' she smiled and carried on, 'Focus and learn to remember quotes accurately. Otherwise you will forever look foolish.'

'I am always accurate Pearl, at least when I need to be.'

'Maybe, but not with this quote. Alexander Graham Bell said, "Concentrate all your thoughts upon the work in hand. The sun's rays do not burn until brought to a focus." He did not say what you just said.'

'Close enough,' said Hilda, shrugging. 'Now to the important things.' Hilda waved at the clue board and said, 'Father Christmas or rather his dead helper.'

'I think a cup of tea will help me think,' said Pearl.

She popped off to make one. Hilda watched her go and then turned back to the clue board. The centre of the board had the word "Father Christmas". Under it were the words, "Not the real one." Then around these words, lines of wool lead out to suspects. None had proper names of actual suspects. They said things like, "Drugs?"

Hilda had put the word "drugs," because the marquess had overheard an argument that could have been about drugs. Whilst drug use was not as widespread in 1948 as in later years in the UK. There was still a problem related to their use. The

Dangerous Drugs Act of 1920 and laws added in 1928 meant that opium, cocaine, and cannabis were illegal. Criminal gangs used existing addictions and encouraged new addictions to these drugs. This level of information was unknown to Hilda. She just felt in her water that drugs might be involved. They sometimes were in the Holywood movies she watched. Not that she really understood why. It had always seemed odd to her that the police arrested gangs of drugs dealers, and yet there were drugstores on the street corners. Nevertheless, she knew that drugs must be a likely lead in the murder. So she circled the word 'drugs.'

On another string Hilda wrote, "Random."

Hilda wanted to cover the possibility that the man in the red suit had just been in the wrong place at the wrong time. Her pops always said to her, 'Be careful Hildy, there are bad people out there.'

She knew bad things just happened to good people. But she hoped that wasn't the case here. Not to Father Christmas, not at this time of year. If it really was a random act by a random person, then it would be almost impossible to solve.

There was another string where Hilda wrote, "Family."

Could it be a pre-meditated murder by a wife, brother, son? Maybe for jealousy, inheritance, or revenge? Had Father Christmas' helper cheated on his wife? Then she had killed him or had him killed. What a terrible thought. This all brought Hilda back to an issue that Scotland Yard had also run into. Who was Father Christmas? Not the real one. We all know who he is. He's St Nicholas, and he lives in the North Pole with a bunch of elves... anyway, that's not the point. Who was the man in the red suit who had been murdered outside Carvey Michaels Department Store? Chief Inspector Loughty had put the full investigative force of Scotland Yard on that very question. So far, they had drawn a blank. Perhaps Hilda could do better.

One last line led to the words, "Gang murder."

Hilda had seen many American movies and understood that criminal gangs also existed outside of America. So she wanted to include the possibility that a gang he was part of had killed the murder victim. She started imagining gangs of Father Christmasses all carrying water pistols, running into shops and firing spurts of magic dust. Then they held out their empty sacks and shouted, 'Fill em up.'

The naughty Father Christmasses then ran out with full sacks and leapt into their sleighs. Pearl brought Hilda back to reality, saying, 'Tea.'

'Never mind the tea,' said Hilda, 'I've got it.'

'That was quick,' said Pearl.

'Aren't you going to ask?' said Hilda.

Pearl put the tray on the top of a chest of drawers and said, 'No, you'll tell me.'

'Oh, that's disappointing,' said Hilda. 'Well, we need to go to Scotland Yard.'

'Why?' asked Pearl.

'Because, I've solved the mystery,' said Hilda.

'Do you think they'll let us in?' asked Pearl.

But she was talking to an empty room. Hilda had already headed off to fetch her coat. Pearl reluctantly followed.

SIS, Whitehall, London, UK

While Hilda was having her eureka moment; her husband Arthur had arrived back at his office in Whitehall. SIS only had a skeleton staff on a Saturday, making the office feel empty. Arthur had phoned ahead and asked to meet Bert. The two men were now sitting staring into his warm fire. He had two comfortable chairs on either side of it. Much preferable to his desk. Arthur said, 'Now I have all the evidence, can we make a move?'

'We had the police raid the warehouse and take the weapons and explosives. They made it look like a random check. That way it won't spoil the rest of our surveillance. But, Jameson wants to wait before we move in on the gang itself,' said Bert.

'I'm glad they at least took the ammo dump out of action,' said Arthur. 'But did he say why he's holding back on the main group?'

Bert glanced up at Arthur and said, 'It's above your level.'

'But they're at the Astoria now, if we don't move immediately, we'll miss them,' said Arthur. 'No matter how subtle the police were. They're bound to realise something's up. Pavlov isn't stupid.'

Arthur got up and paced around, arms behind his back. Bert looked at his son-in-law and said, 'That's the frustration of being a junior agent. You have to follow orders and assume those above you know best. There's a bigger picture here other things going on.'

Arthur stopped and stared at Bert. 'Do you know that bigger picture? I know you can't tell me the details. But if you know it. Please say if you agree with it.'

Bert gazed into the fire and took a deep breath. Then, looking deeply into Arthur's eyes, he said, 'I don't know everything, but I trust Jameson.'

'That's good enough for me,' said Arthur, then he headed out of the office and home. As Bert watched Arthur leave, he whispered to himself, 'How can I disagree with my boss? I really hope he knows what he's doing.'

Hilda's home, Kilburn, UK

'I'm home love,' shouted Arthur as he opened the front door.

All was silent in response. No notes on the side. But then Hilda would not have expected Arthur home so early. He had told her he was away all weekend, at least. Still, he felt disappointed. Arthur contemplated searching for his wife at Pearl's house. But then gave her a while to return first. He took his case upstairs. As he passed the spare bedroom, he could see inside. A large board on the wall displayed details about the murder of the man who played Father Christmas a few weeks ago. Arthur walked into the room. Hilda had ringed a name and written, 'Guilty!'

He realised where Hilda might be. They didn't have a phone in their home, so Arthur went out to a local phone box and made a couple of phone calls.

Scotland Yard, London, UK

Hilda and Pearl danced into Scotland Yard. In reality, only Hilda was dancing. Pearl crept slowly behind her. The entrance lobby was crowded, and everyone turned to stare at the dancing interloper; she made quite an entrance. Hilda took a bow, and the opportunity afforded by the distraction to gain a place at the front of the queue. Everyone had turned away from the reception desk to see what was happening. Pearl followed Hilda and apologised to everyone who had now realised they had been overtaken. Hilda bowed to those in the queue and the desk sergeant and then said, 'We are here to see Chief Inspector Dafty.'

The desk sergeant stifled a laugh and said, 'I think you mean Loughty.' He then phoned through to the chief inspector. 'I have two young ladies here for you sir.'

'What are their names and why are they here?' asked Loughty on the phone.

The desk sergeant spoke to Hilda and Pearl and then said to Loughty, 'It's a Mrs Shilton and Miss...'

'I don't want to see them,' cut in Loughty.

'Mrs Shilton says she has important information that will solve the case of the dead Father Christmas... oh, she added not the real one.'

'What information?' asked Loughty.

'Hang on a minute sir, Sergeant Humblecut has just arrived back and is talking to them, I'll let him deal with it,' said the desk sergeant. He hung up.

'Hello, hello,' shouted Loughty down the phone.

In the chief inspector's office, Loughty banged the phone down.

***

Ten minutes later, the door of Chief Inspector Loughty's office opened and in walked Sergeant Humblecut with Hilda and Pearl. Hilda took a quick look around the room, spotted Loughty behind his desk, strode up to him and said, 'I've solved it for you.'

'Humble, what are you doing bringing these two... these... girls in here?' shouted Loughty.

'I beg your pardon,' said Hilda. 'You need to mind your manners. Being a great clothing detective doesn't give you the right to insult young ladies.'

Loughty stood up; an imposing sight. He took a deep breath. His cheeks were a wonderful shade of red. Perhaps he was practicing to be a Father Christmas helper? Just before he could shout, the commissioner of Scotland Yard walked in and said, 'Ah, I see Mrs Shilton is here as expected.'

Loughty glanced between the commissioner and Hilda, then said, 'Yes sir.'

'I'm glad to see that. I just had her husband, Arthur, on the phone. He has a very important and hush, hush, job at Whitehall. He was looking for his wife, then realised she may have come here. So I assured him that we would obviously be treating Mrs Shilton with full respect. That's right, isn't it chief inspector?'

'Of course sir,' said Loughty, deflated. He sat down. 'Mrs Shilton was just about to share her theories...'

'Facts,' said Hilda.

'Facts,' said Loughty, glaring at Hilda. 'About a recent murder.'

'Good, good,' said the commissioner. 'Well, I'll leave it in your capable hands. Make sure you treat her right, eh what. I'll check back later.'

***

It was a short time later that Hilda, Pearl, Loughty, and Humblecut were sitting in Loughty's office. Hilda found sitting a trial, so she sprang to her feet and did a twirl. Then stood in the middle of the room, ready to explain how Father Christmas had been murdered. 'Twas the night before Christmas and all through the house,' said Hilda.

'Hold on,' said Loughty. 'What are you talking about?'

Hilda smiled and said, 'A friend of mine from America sent me this delightful poem all about the night before Christmas.'

'But Mrs Shilton,' said Sergeant Humblecut. 'The murder victim didn't die on Christmas Eve.'

'So he didn't,' said Hilda. 'What a pity, it would have worked very well with my poem.'

'Why's that Mrs Shilton?' asked Humblecut.

'Did you take a careful look at the body?' Humblecut nodded. Hilda continued, 'Well in the poem it says that Father Christmas "...looked like a pedler just opening his pack." Then a line further on it says, "His cheeks were like roses, his nose like a cherry!" and a line or two later, "And the beard of his chin was as white as the snow..." you see that describes the man we all saw.'

'Could be anyone,' said Loughty, snorting.

'I assume you still haven't found out who the dead man is?' asked Hilda.

'Nothing much to go on,' said Humblecut.

As he was speaking, there was a knock on the door and Loughty shouted for them to come in. An officer entered and said, 'I've got the marquess for you sir.'

'I didn't...' started Loughty.

'Oh, sorry sir,' cut in Humblecut. 'Mrs Shilton asked if he could join us. She explained it was important. I hope that's alright?'

'Why not, who am I to have a say in my own investigation?' said Loughty crossly.

'Remember your own commissioner,' said Hilda, smiling at Loughty. He frowned.

The Marquess of Messex entered and said, 'So glad to be of service ladies.' He tipped his hat at Hilda and Pearl. Then noticed Loughty and Humblecut, 'And gentlemen.'

They gave the marquess a seat next to Pearl and Humblecut. Hilda still stood in the middle of the room. She said, 'Now we're all here. As I was saying the Father Christmas we found dead had rosy cheeks and a red nose. They also had a big bushy white beard; quite unkempt. Something we all expect of such a person.' Everyone nodded, except Loughty, he snorted. Hilda continued, 'Except, normally a person playing that part uses makeup and a beard.'

'There are people with big bushy beards you know,' said Loughty. 'They can even have red noses and rosy cheeks.'

He looked around for agreement. But only received a few half nods. 'Of course,' said Hilda. 'But it got me thinking and I don't give up on and idea once I have it. As Churchill said,

"Never give in, never give in, never, never," there were a lot of nevers. My point is that when I get a bee in my bonnet about something I don't let it go.'

'That's very true,' said Pearl.

'Where are you going with this?' asked Loughty.

'I thought this, what if the Father Christmas was not Father Christmas? I know he wasn't really Father Christmas. But what if someone dressed him up to be Father Christmas. Someone with a wicked sense of humour. It was the week before Christmas after all and they saw the mans red face and white beard and thought, "He looks like Father Christmas." So they disguised him.'

'But why would anyone do that?' asked Loughty.

'Think about where the body was found,' said Hilda. 'The alley at the side of Carvey Michaels Department Store. I assume you've checked where it goes and looked at the entrances off that alleyway chief inspector?'

Chief Inspector Loughty looked shocked for a moment, then turned to his sergeant and said, 'That was your job Humble. I assume you checked that thoroughly?'

'Yes sir,' said Humblecut, smiling. 'I've had a chat with Mrs Shilton about this already; she had some good ideas on that.'

Loughty glanced between his sergeant and Hilda. He looked like a man at a tennis match. Hilda then said, 'Your sergeant found the same as myself. That alley is used as a drop off point by a criminal gang. They use it everyday. It's a hotbed of criminal activity. You really ought to have policemen there. Anyway, one day, an unfortunate homeless man decided to take up residence there and caught them red handed, so to speak.'

Loughty turned to the marquess and said, 'My dear man, I am so sorry for you. You saw these criminals murder the Father Christmas?'

Hilda shook her head and said to the marquess, 'That would seem the obvious answer and indeed is what you planned, isn't it?' Then she turned to Loughty and said, 'But no, that's not what I'm saying. The marquess here, was caught in the act by the homeless man. Then the marquess murdered that poor man. He dressed up the homeless man as Father Christmas and took his place.'

The marquess had been watching Hilda, wide eyed. He now said, 'I have no idea what you're talking about.'

Hilda stared at the marquess and said, 'When did Lucian blackmail you into working for him?'

Loughty had been open-mouthed during this exchange. He shouted, 'What's the matter with you woman? Accusing a peer of the realm. I don't care what the commissioner says. Get out of my office.' He then turned to the marquess and said, 'I am sorry my lord. If there's anything I can do?'

'Just get rid of this ridiculous woman,' said the marquess. He was red faced. 'Accusing me of murder, she must be mad.'

Humblecut escorted Hilda and Pearl from the building. Whilst he agreed with Hilda about her conclusions; he was unable to go against his boss. He tried speaking to the commissioner. But when he explained that a marquess had been accused of the murder with no actual evidence; Humblecut received a verbal warning from the commissioner.

Back at home, Hilda told Arthur all about her dreadful day and the fact she was sure that The Marquess of Messex was guilty of murder. She explained he had then dressed the body as Father Christmas and stayed at the scene pretending to be a homeless man. She just needed proof. Arthur sat, listening in silence. He had the proof his wife needed at SIS headquarters. The diary and the ledger gave physical proof of the payments to the marquess. This would show he was being blackmailed by Lucian Kendall. The ledger also showed details of the criminal activities that happened in that alley by Carvey Michael's store. But now, they had classified it as top secret. This was one of Arthur's worst days.

CHAPTER TWELVE

April 1st 2005

Hidden Garden Tearooms

Plympton-on-Sea, UK

Fifty-seven years later, Hilda had just solved a case that involved a vicar being killed. It had seemed impossible. The vicar had dropped dead in his pulpit for no obvious reason. The post mortem could find no cause of death natural or caused by others. But in the end Hilda solved it.

Hilda always liked to celebrate the end of a case. The Hanley case was no different. So she sent out invites for a party. But she chose April 1st. Which meant that everyone assumed it was a joke. Several people she invited didn't turn up, because they were sure it was a trick. But all of Hilda's close family and friends came. They knew it was typical of her. Pearl made a special effort and hopped on a plane from the USA to be with her. She was finding Florida very hot and humid. Ruby was used to Washington DC and besides, she had a lot of social activities, so she stayed in America. Annie and Peter, Hilda's American friends, had to give their apologies because it was a busy time at work and flights from America were not cheap. Chief Inspector York, the detective on the Hanley case, brought his now fiance, Yvonne Hanley. Hilda was sure she'd receive an invitation to the wedding and so she wanted them at her party. Sergeant Ilari Batra, York's sergeant, brought her sister. She explained she was far too busy with work to bother with dating. Just as with Hilda's last party, Lauren, and Kelly, the current tearoom owners, hired in staff to do the work so that they could attend. Ex-PM the Rt Hon Nicholas Martin spared time from his busy schedule running an international computing business to attend.

However, it wasn't the ex-PM who caused the biggest stir at the party; he was only a retired politician. Rather, it was the duchess of Somershire, Jayne Milford. In 2005, she was a duchess. The guests were very impressed that Hilda was friends with a member of the nobility. But the duchess only came after Hilda told her it was a fundraiser. On arrival Jayne discovered Hilda had meant a fun raiser, but she stayed on anyway. Jayne enjoyed a bit of fun.

***

By late afternoon, the party was in full swing, and everyone was enjoying themselves. The Duchess of Somershire even danced with her old friend Nicholas Martin; the ex-PM of the UK.

Sergeant Ilari's sister was getting bored. 'This isn't really my thing Lari,' she said.

'We'll give it another five minutes, then go and find a film to watch,' said Ilari.

The sergeant checked her bag to make sure she had enough cash to fulfil her promise. There were two small books half-hidden at the bottom. She took them out, remembering why she'd put them there. 'Hang on a sec,' she said to her sister.

Ilari headed over to her boss, Inspector York, and said, 'We were going to give these to Mrs Shilton.'

'Of course, the books Professor Price had in her flat. Is this the right time?' asked York.

Professor Price was a history professor researching the UK secret service. In her research, she had unearthed things that helped the investigation into the Rev Hanley case. But also found these two books.

Ilari glanced at the books and over towards Hilda, then said to York, 'Pearl heads back to the USA soon, Mrs Shilton might want to give the diary to her.'

'I'll let you decide,' said York.

A few minutes later Hilda was sitting reading the two books and notes. Victoria Kendall nee Worth had written the diary. She was Pearl, and Ruby's natural mother. The ledger contained financial information and belonged to Lucian Kendall. On their own, the diary and ledger were confusing. But with the SIS code breakers notes, they became clear. After reading for a while, Hilda looked up and said, 'This gives me the proof I needed for a murder back in 1948.'

'What murder?' asked Ilari.

'The murder of Father Christmas,' said Hilda.

'Eh?' said Ilari.

'Well obviously not the real one,' said Hilda. 'He lives in the North Pole.'

'Can we just back up here a minute,' said Ilari. 'You were involved in a murder case back in 1948?'

'Yes dear, One of Santas helpers. He was standing outside a department store in London. Or rather he was murdered outside it.'

'You'll have to explain a bit more,' said Ilari.

'I will,' said Hilda. 'But first, I think Pearl would love to read the diary of her mother. At least the less traumatic bits.'

***

After Pearl read her mother's diary. Hilda explained the importance of the two books. First everything that we have heard. Then Hilda said, 'It was so frustrating to be kicked out of Scotland Yard. I realised that The Marquess of Messex was working for Lucian Kendall's organisation. I just couldn't prove it; until now. Do you know that I found these books all those years ago?'

'Then how come they were with MI6?' asked Pearl, looking up from her mother's diary.

'Obviously I didn't know who Victoria was and that other book was a complete mystery. You know what I'm like with numbers Pearl.' Her friend nodded. 'So I just put the two books on my bookshelf. I have no idea how they ended up...' Hilda had a startled look on her face. 'Of course, my dearest Arthur worked with pops.'

'What did your pops do?' asked Ilari.

'He had a top secret job,' said Hilda. 'I never fully knew. Something or other to do with spying. I only found out that Arthur was also a spy a few years ago. He must have found the books and seen Victoria's name. Or rather her surname, Kendall. That's why he was killed dear, because of Lucian Kendall. He must have been investigating Lucian Kendall even in 1948.' Hilda shook her head sadly. Pearl got up and gave her friend a hug.

'How does all this prove that The Marquess of Messex was guilty of the murder though?' asked Ilari.

Hilda took a deep breath and said, 'The code breakers have made the ledger easy to read and linked it to the diary. So that I can now make sense of it. With what I knew at the time, it all makes sense. The ledger is full of initials, dates, and numbers. The code breakers say that these are people paid on certain dates an amount of money. They have worked out who is who by cross referencing the people Victoria talks about in the diary. People who Lucian and she visited or who came to the house. These are the key bits:'

- **GMM is Gerald the Marquess of Messex**

- **MLV the Maid of Lady Vernon**

- **AJK the hotel Astoria John Keighley**

'There are amounts of money by each. Payments in red they assumed meant owed and the subject is being blackmailed. That was the case with the marquess. He owed a lot of money to their organisation. Lady Vernon's maid had a small payment, no doubt for information. Lord Veron was a cabinet minister. So no doubt she would pass information on to Lucian. John Keighley became Lucian Kendall's replacement after he moved across to the USA. But at the time of the ledger he was down as collecting debts for Lucian. For that he received a regular cut.'

'Yes, but how does this prove that the marquess was the murderer?' asked Ilari.

'First you need to know that the Father Christmas we found dead had red cheeks and nose and a big bushy white beard; quite unkempt,' said Hilda.

'What's unusual about that?' asked Ilari. 'Wasn't he playing Santa?'

'That's why everyone ignored it,' said Hilda. 'But normally people dressing up as Santa's helpers have to use makeup, don't they?'

Everyone nodded. A few people looked uncertain. Perhaps they knew a few people who looked just like Santa. Ilari said, 'That's hardly proof.'

'That was my problem at the time. It was odd, but not proof. But it did get me thinking. What if our Father Christmas was actually a homeless man with a drinking problem? His red cheeks and nose were the burst blood vessels caused by too much alcohol. The unkempt beard due to a lack of shaving. I asked Sergeant Humblecut, one of the officers, about the post mortem. The doctor had commented on how unclean the body had been.'

'Pointers, but to what?' asked Ilari.

'What if our Father Christmas had been a homeless man lying in the alley when something happened there? He witnessed it. Then the people he saw spotted him and decided to get rid of him; permanently. Imagine that this homeless man had witnessed Father Christmas himself up to no good. So this poor man gets up and goes over to Father Christmas and challenges him. But of course it's not Father Christmas but a criminal using that disguise. This criminal murders the homeless man and dresses him up in the Father Christmas outfit. Then takes his place. Pretending to be homeless. That way he can observe the police investigation. But also carry on with his activities in that alleyway.'

'That's why The Marquess of Messex is listed in the book?' asked Ilari. 'He worked for Lucian?'

'Yes,' said Hilda. 'He was in that alley, using a Father Christmas disguise he met his criminal contacts. The homeless man challenged him. The marquess murdered him and dressed him in the outfit. Then took his place.'

'But you lacked any physical evidence, until now,' said Ilari. 'No DNA, no written evidence. What about fingerprints?'

'The police investigation at the time was poor and the chief inspector was unwilling to look at a marquess,' said Hilda.

'Different times,' said Ilari.

'Yes indeed dear,' said Hilda.

'I wonder if we can re-open the case?' asked Ilari.

'The Marquess of Messex is dead,' said Hilda. 'Lucian Kendall had him killed for stealing from him. I followed his activities from a distance over the years. So I guess justice was done. But it's still good to have proof that I was right.'

Pearl smiled at her friend. Ilari shook her head and headed off to find her sister. Who she found sitting chatting with William and Louise.

The party was in full swing, and everyone was enjoying themselves. Pearl had a sip of her drink then said to Hilda, 'Do you fancy joining Ruby and I in Florida for Christmas?'

'I'd love to dear,' said Hilda. 'It's always so chilly here.'

***

A while later, William brought sergeant Ilari and her sister back over to Hilda. Louise followed. William said, 'Tell the sergeant that I did run past a dead body as a teenager.'

'What's that?' asked Hilda.

He stared hard at Hilda and said, 'Mother, you remember, that dead body I kept running past.'

'You, running,' said Hilda. She glanced at Pearl and said, 'The things our children come up with.' Pearl shrugged. Hilda then said to William, 'I don't ever remember you running.'

William shook his head in exasperation. The rest of the group, with William, now sat down to join Hilda and Pearl. William stayed standing. Sergeant Ilari said, 'I thought it sounded a bit implausible.'

'It was true,' said William. 'A shocking experience it was after they found the body.'

Hilda screwed up her face and said, 'Do you mean that young lady who was murdered in the 1960's?'

'I think it was in the sixties, I guess I'd be about fifteen or sixteen,' said William. 'But the key bit is that I ran past the body for a few weeks.'

Hilda frowned and pursed her lips, then said, 'Ah yes, that case. I remember now. As usual the police needed my help to solve it.'

Sergeant Ilari sighed. William looked fit to burst and said, 'What about me?'

'Yes, you did run past the body in the ditch one week, or maybe two.'

Louise glanced between her husband and Hilda and said, 'Now this is a story I've never heard.'

'Really?' said Hilda. 'Perhaps we all need a drink and I should tell you about the Somershire Murders.'

The End

Hilda will return in: Book 8 – Somershire Murders.

If you enjoyed this book, please leave an honest review.

Character List

Main Characters

Hilda and *Arthur* Shilton UK
*Hilda is 28 at the beginning of the book.
Arthur works for SIS*

Pearl Parker (UK)
Pearl is Hilda's best friend

Bert & Henrietta (UK)
*Hilda's Father (Pops) and Mother
Bert works for SIS*

Ron and Eileen (UK)
Pearls Parents

Victoria Kendall Nee Worth
Pearl & Ruby's natural mother

Scotland Yard

Chief Inspector Loughty (UK)

Sergeant Humblecut (UK)

SIS (Secret Intelligence Service)

Commander Jameson
Head of SIS

Other

Lord & Lady John & Virginia Vernon (UK)
Lady Vernon has her gloves stolen

Lucian Kendall
Head of criminal organisation

Penelope Kendall
Lucian's daughter
Pearl & Ruby's half sister

John Keighley
Lucian's right-hand man
Manager of Astoria

Jayne Bulsam
Later becomes, Duchess of Somershire
Friend of Penelope Kendall

Marquess of Messex (UK)
Homeless man in alley

ALSO BY MIKE NEVIN

Book 1 Diamonds of Death
Book 2 Teacakes and Murder
Book 3 Millennium Mystery
Book 4: Double Dealing
Book 5: Death in a Churchyard
Book 6: Death in a Pulpit

Check out my website at Howcaring.com for the latest news. My Email address is: mike@thenevins.org.uk

Find my Books Here:

About the Author

I'm married with three children. A Londoner by birth, though we've lived in most parts of the UK. Two of our three children have emigrated to the USA, giving me an insight and love for America. Illness limited my body to a wheelchair in the early 2000s, but gave my mind the freedom to pursue my early passion for writing. To help me develop those skills, I gained a degree in English Lit and a diploma in creative writing.

My main character, Hilda Shilton, expresses a side of me that is bursting to get out. She brings out much of what I admire: tenacity, boldness, strength of character and the ability to go through life not worrying about what others think.

Printed in Great Britain
by Amazon